A DEADLY INDIFFERENCE

A DEADLY INDIFFERENCE

Marshall Jevons

CARROLL & GRAF PUBLISHERS, INC.
New York

First edition 1995.

Carroll & Graf Publishers, Inc.
260 Fifth Avenue
New York, NY 10001

The authors are grateful for permission to reprint lyrics from "This Could Be the Start of Something Big," copyright © Steve Allen.

Library of Congress Cataloging-in-Publication Data

Jevons, Marshall.
    A deadly indifference / Marshall Jevons.—1st ed.
        p.   cm.
    ISBN 0-7867-0200-1
    I. Title.
PS3560.E88D4   1995
813'.54—dc20   95-6852
                                                          CIP

Manufactured in the United States of America

A Note to the Reader

    Although *A Deadly Indifference* is Marshall Jevons's third Henry Spearman novel, the action it chronicles takes place earler than did the first two. This adventure takes place in the mid-1960s. But it is not a younger Henry Spearman who appears in these pages. Unlike Agatha Christie's Hercule Poirot, Henry Spearman does not age. More like Rex Stout's Nero Wolfe, Henry Spearman is timeless. This literary license allows the author to avoid some inconveniences that might otherwise encumber the story.

Tiger Tiger, burning bright,
In the forests of the night;
What immortal hand or eye,
Could frame thy fearful symmetry?

William Blake
"Songs of Experience"

A DEADLY INDIFFERENCE

Chapter 1:
Remains to Be Seen

London 1965

The lone occupant of the mahogany case stared impassively from behind the glass at his two visitors. Hurrying students, on their way to class, were heedless of the enclosed figure. The box's resident returned the compliment. He had a good excuse. He was dead.

"He *does* look a lot like Benjamin Franklin," Henry Spearman commented to his wife as he stepped back from the brown wooden case to get a better perspective.

The corpse, which had the rapt attention of Pidge and Henry Spearman, was the mortal remains of the English jurist and philosopher, Jeremy Bentham. The resemblance to Benjamin Franklin was striking. England's great economist, David Ricardo, had noted it during Bentham's own lifetime. When Ricardo encountered a bust of Franklin in a sculptor's shop while vacationing in Italy, he wrote home, "It must be a bargain because it answers the object of two busts." Ricardo made the purchase.

The macabre display had deflected the Spearmans from going from Boston straight to their destination at Cambridge. Instead, they decided to take the time to visit University College, London, on that April morning. Bentham's remains were, after all, the closest thing economists had to an Epiphany. Bentham called it the Auto-Icon.

Jeremy Bentham's will had stipulated that his body was to be

1

given to his friend, Dr. Southwood Smith, for immortalization. The instructions were explicit: "The skeleton he will cause to be put together in such manner as that the whole figure may be seated in a chair usually occupied by me when I am engaged in thought. He will cause the skeleton to be clad in one of the suits of black occasionally worn by me." The Spearmans read these words from the portion of the will attached to the door of the movable mausoleum.

More students scurried by. Henry Spearman was amused by their total indifference to the presence of the preserved body. A stuffed moose head on the wall might have elicited more interest from them.

A wry smile crossed Pidge Spearman's lips. Her voice tinged with irony, she intoned; "I don't think he's having the effect he intended."

"What did he expect? It was a bad idea to begin with." The sarcastic remark at first surprised the Spearmans. Unbeknownst to Pidge and Henry, another couple behind them also had been studying the Auto-Icon. The young woman who had spoken was wearing a lavender shirtwaist dress and matching hat.

Spearman's face lit up. He seized his opportunity. "It was not a bad idea to a utilitarian like Bentham," he said with a smile. "You can see how someone who lived his life according to the principle of 'the greatest happiness to the greatest number' might have come up with it. After all, why not make better use of the dead than burying or cremating them? Bentham's idea was to put the stuffed bodies of all the great people on permanent display. That would provide more inspiration for future generations than stone markers in cemeteries." Henry Spearman turned to face the newcomers and smiled broadly.

"Wouldn't a statue have done the trick? At least then his clothes wouldn't look so seedy." These remarks came from the gentleman standing next to the young woman. His disapproval of Bentham's dishevelment was a reflection of his own grooming and attire. He was the kind of man who wears a navy blazer with a family crest and doesn't look foppish doing so.

Bentham's attire did show signs of wear after decades of encasement. His trousers were moth-eaten. His straw hat and gloves looked more like those of a gardener than a scholar. Only his waistcoat and lace collar conveyed the impression of an English man of letters. His once fashionable walking stick lay diagonally across his lap.

Spearman replied with a wave of his hand toward the figure behind the glass door. "A statue would miss the mark. Bentham wanted people to see him as he really was. It was the sense of his presence that was to inspire his disciples. Notice how the inner case is on casters. When Benthamites have meetings to discuss his ideas, they simply wheel the Auto-Icon into the meeting room—just as Bentham stipulated in his will."

Pidge looked embarrassed. "You'll have to forgive my husband. He's a professor and will give a lecture whenever he thinks he has a student. It's an occupational hazard," Pidge said to the twosome, with a look of feigned apology on her face. To her, Bentham's remains were anything but inspirational. They reminded her that even the lives of great people end in death and decay.

"There's nothing to forgive," the older gentleman said to Pidge and her husband. "We're delighted to have the information. I had heard about this display from a business associate of mine, but I never actually understood what it was all about. Now I do, thanks to . . .?"

"I'm Henry Spearman. And this is my wife, Pidge."

"A pleasure, I'm sure. My name is Graham Carlton, and this is my friend, Ardis Horne. We were in the neighborhood of the College, so we stopped off to see Bentham for ourselves. The old boy did have a point, didn't he? And the wax museums seem to have got it."

"What do you mean?" Henry asked.

"Well, look at the success of places like Madame Tussaud's. People will pay to see resemblances of the dead. Maybe somebody should move this old boy over there. At least he'd get some attention."

"I think Jeremy Bentham would have a hard time competing with Henry VIII and Elizabeth Taylor," Ardis quipped. "He was the College's greatest benefactor, but he doesn't seem to be able to get the attention of any students. And there's not even any ticket price to pay here."

Graham Carlton glanced at his watch and then at his companion. "Well, I think we've seen what we came to see, Ardis." He turned to the Spearmans. "Thank you for the lecture, Professor. It's been a pleasure meeting you both. Do enjoy your stay in England." With that, the couple moved in the direction of the exit.

The South Cloisters of University College's once-crowded hallways were almost empty. The next round of classes at the University College had begun. It was clear that the young scholars would be taught without any inspiration from Jeremy Bentham's Auto-Icon.

Chapter 2:
Train to Cambridge

The train from the Liverpool Station left precisely on schedule, sliding past the warehouses, flats, and factories at increasing speed. The clickety-clack of the wheels made a barely audible hum as the train picked up momentum. Its speed soon matched the pace of the fastest-moving cars on the A10 near Edmonton, outside London. Urban landscape gave way to the lush farmlands of East Anglia.

Whump! A fast-moving train from the opposite direction hurtled past the windows of the Spearmans' coach. The rushing noise changed the air pressure enough to cause eardrums to vibrate.

"Tickets, tickets, please." A fiftyish, rusty-haired, chunky man, made his way down the aisle.

"Will you let us know when we've reached Cambridge?" Henry Spearman inquired.

"Oh, you'll know that, sir. You'll know that without my telling you. The train terminates at Cambridge. If you don't get off at Cambridge, you'll be the only ones left on it."

Henry Spearman sat back and relaxed. He and Pidge knew that British Railways did not dally long at a station. Traveling to the end of the line meant one did not have to watch for station signs or listen for the conductor's call. As Pidge looked in her handbag she said, "Henry, would you go over the schedule once we get to Cambridge?"

Henry Spearman was a short man with twinkling gray eyes and a nearly bald head. His wife, Pidge, was a lively, buxom woman with an earnest manner. He was a professor of economics at Harvard. She had been raised in an academic family. Pidge and Henry Spearman had met as undergraduates at Columbia, where Henry had stayed on for his doctorate. Since joining the Harvard faculty, his reputation had grown rapidly. He was an academic hot property, best known for developing new applications of economic theory for the most commonplace activities.

Spearman turned from the window and pulled a calendar from his breast pocket. "Well, we should arrive in Cambridge around ten o'clock today. We'll check in at our hotel, get a bite to eat, and then we have the afternoon to ourselves. I thought we might play tourist and look around Cambridge. I can't tell how much time I'll have for that sort of thing after today. Tomorrow morning, at nine, I meet with Morris Fain and Duncan Thring at Marshall's house. I hope you can come along for that. Then Jared wants to take us to lunch."

Spearman paused for a moment and went on: "Later in the afternoon, I'll be having tea with some of his colleagues. So you're on your own. Morris Fain wants to take you for a drive around the area. He was stationed here during the war and wants to visit some of his old haunts. In any event I doubt if you'd want to sit through my lecture. You've heard most of it before. My talk is in the late afternoon, so we can meet later at the hotel and get ready to attend a cocktail party in my honor hosted by some members of the economics faculty. Then we'll have a late dinner together, maybe at the hotel.

"Friday is a bit unclear, depending on how the negotiations go with Thring. There's nothing planned on the weekend. Monday may be needed for legal work and details. I hope we can leave Tuesday with the deed to a new house."

A perceptible decrease in the train's speed caused the Spearmans to glance out the window. As their car pulled alongside a station platform, a signpost reading "Audley End" came into view. Spearman examined his timetable, running his eyes down the London-Cambridge column. "About fifteen more minutes and we should be there."

The Spearmans looked around. They were on a mid-morning,

off-peak run of the train to Cambridge. They noticed their car was now empty except for one open-jawed young man at the rear whose head, cocked back in sleep, emitted a rhythmic snore. As the train resumed its forward motion and gained momentum, its sounds muffled those of the slumberer. Unlike the Spearmans, their fellow passenger was oblivious to the passing countryside and the flat earth spreading out uninterrupted to the horizon.

Pidge Spearman returned to a Dorothy Sayers paperback she had nearly completed. Her husband, seated across from her, was preoccupied with thoughts of the responsibility that awaited him in Cambridge. It was one thing to buy a house for yourself, but quite another to make such a major purchase for someone else. When the foundation first approached him, he said no, hoping that someone more experienced in such matters would go instead. Then he was asked again. Professor Wolk, the man Spearman had recommended, had accepted at first, and then became ill. The foundation's entreaties to Spearman were successful the second time.

For one thing, both Spearmans were invited to go. Pidge was enthusiastic about the trip. "Why not accept?" she had asked. "We've never been to Cambridge together. That could be fun—King's College Chapel, the Bridge of Sighs. You could see your old friend, Jared McDonald. And we could see the Bentham display in London, something you know you always wanted to do. Anyway, it could be a nice vacation for us."

If Pidge had not been along, Henry would have felt less certain about closing a deal. She had a keen eye for real estate. His wife could see a house as it is; she could also see it as it could be. And her instincts about people were good. Better than his, he had to admit.

Pidge's abilities were especially useful in the purchase of used goods, where the current owner knows an item inside out and the prospective purchaser doesn't. As an economist, Henry Spearman recognized that one of the problems with market economies was that buyers often had less information about a product than sellers. As a consequence, higher-quality goods often never made their way into the market. Owners of well-cared-for products—like good used cars or lawnmowers—had incentives to seek out friends as purchasers rather than peddle their possessions in the marketplace, where their things might be assessed as having the same value as lower-quality items of the same type. Pidge's presence would help offset the asymmetry in knowledge which Henry would have in contrast to the property's owner.

Watching her read as the train rolled on, he thought about how lucky he was to be married to her. She appeared to him almost the same as she had fifteen years ago when they were married. The same chestnut hair, the same light complexion, and the soft brown eyes that attracted him to her so many years ago—they attracted him still. Only the fine lines at the corner of her eyes and the set of her firm chin indicated her maturity. She was taller than he—something her father never failed to point out when they were dating. But if it mattered to her, she never revealed it.

Their dating pattern had been unusual. Pidge always wondered if others who dated people trained in economics encountered the same situation. The peculiarity involved the social tradition of the male paying for the date, and the economic theory of gifts and transfer payments.

Henry Spearman knew from economic analysis that if a person were offered $100 cash, or as an alternative, an assortment of goods worth one hundred dollars selected randomly or chosen by someone else, the recipient generally would be better off taking the cash and spending it on the goods and services the *recipient* selects. Another party rarely would have the knowledge to select the bundle of goods worth one hundred dollars that would maximize the individual's economic satisfaction, or what Spearman called "utility."

The economic theory of the consumer rests on an individual maximizing his or her utility by purchasing more of this and less of that. The same principle could apply to a gift or payment from the Government: only the recipient had the knowledge and the incentives to spend the money to generate the most satisfaction. For that person, gifts-in-kind were inefficient. This is why many economists support direct cash grants to the poor, rather than have government relief agencies offer non-cash material assistance.

Henry Spearman had applied this economic principle to courting Pidge. He would invite Pidge out, say to a movie and dessert afterwards. In the same conversation, Spearman would offer Pidge the alternative of taking the cash equivalent of what he would have spent on her. He was quite transparent in offering Pidge the cash alternative. His reasoning had two elements.

First, Spearman recognized all too well that Pidge was free to take the money and run. By choosing a different set of goods and services than the date with Henry, Pidge might be able to get a greater amount of satisfaction. Second, Henry Spearman knew that if he really loved Pidge, he would want her to be as happy as possible, even if that meant not having her company. He maintained that putting their welfare first, offering someone the cash equivalent of a date, was a sure sign of genuine love for the other person.

Henry had told Pidge more than once before they were married that love, to an economist, was a matter of interdependent utility functions. Interdependent utility functions were the very essence of love: one receives pleasure giving the other person pleasure. With all that's written about love, Spearman did not know of a songwriter who had ever picked up on this theme. But he thought this probably was because of the difficulty of getting lyrics to rhyme with "interdependent utility function," and not with the subtlety of the concept.

Only once did Pidge accept the cash equivalent. On that occasion it was more out of curiosity, to see if her boyfriend's economic logic would be backed up by action. It was. Henry Spearman gave her twelve dollars, his estimate of the cost of a dinner and a theatrical production at Columbia. All the other times Pidge accepted Henry's invitations and declined the cash. Henry never considered Pidge's turning down the cash to be irrational on her part. To him, it was a sign of Pidge's utility function being intertwined with his. They were, one might say, falling in love.

"Cam-bridge, Cam-bridge!" The conductor's announcement coincided with the deceleration of the locomotive. "All change! The train terminates here."

The Spearmans rose to gather their baggage. Pidge took two small canvas bags from the overhead rack, while Henry retrieved a Pullman bag from between the seats. Laden down, they began to make their way to the car's exit door.

They stepped to the platform of the Italianate railroad station. Passing through its arcaded loggia, the couple exited on the opposite side of the building where a line of cabs waited. A short taxi ride later, the Spearmans would be ensconced in their Cambridge hotel.

Chapter 3:
Punting on the Cam

Morris Fain felt good to be in England again. For one thing he liked courteous people, and courtesy was a trait in diminishing supply in America. Then there was the predictability. You could count on the trains, the postal service, and the beer. They were consistently excellent. In Chicago, public transportation had deteriorated; the mail had become erratic; and apart from the Hofbrau, if you wanted a decent beer, forget it. In England, it seemed that wherever you went, the personnel knew what they were doing. Not so much buck-passing.

"Would you register, please?" A cordial young man with reddish hair and a freckled face stood at attention behind the front counter of the Blue Boar hotel. He wore a uniform that made him look like Johnny, the bellhop in the Philip Morris ads.

The tall, bespectacled gentleman filled in the appropriate blanks on the form with deliberation. The clerk scanned the information and said, "Is this your first visit, Mr. Fain?"

"My first time with you—my first time in Cambridge, actually. But I do know London a bit. During the war I was stationed in East Anglia. But those were busy times, and I never had a chance to visit here."

"I hope you enjoy the opportunity now, sir. Shall I have you shown to your room?"

"Yes, thank you. Oh, by the way, have the Spearmans from Cambridge—that's Cambridge, Massachusetts—checked in?"

"They haven't checked in yet, sir. But they are booked for today."

"I'd like to leave a message for them," Fain responded.

"Certainly," the registrar replied, placing a sheet of hotel stationery before the guest. Fain drafted a note indicating his safe arrival in Cambridge and confirming that he would join the Spearmans tomorrow as planned. "Let's agree that we should see Balliol Croft for the first time together. Thring expects us in the morning at 9:00 A.M.," he wrote.

"I'd appreciate your seeing that this gets to my friends when they check in," he said, as he sealed the message in an envelope.

The couple Morris Fain awaited was Professor Henry Spearman and his wife, Pidge. The Spearmans were joining him to assist in the project that brought him to England.

Trudging up the stairs at the side of the lobby, Fain was escorted to his lodgings on the second floor overlooking Trinity Street. He went to the window and looked at the busy road below.

"Is the room satisfactory, sir?"

"Everything seems fine," he said as he dismissed the porter, handing him a gratuity. Fain looked around his small room inquisitively. It had that cozy look he associated with English comfort. The room looked settled-in, without being seedy. He removed his suit coat and flopped backwards on to the bed. Typically when he traveled, he did this to test the mattress. But this time it was due to fatigue from the all-night flight to London, and the early morning bus ride to Cambridge from Heathrow.

Refreshed after a short nap, Fain unpacked his bags, showered, dressed himself in khakis, a blue cotton sport shirt, and some walking shoes. Later there would be business to do, but first he would spend some time as a tourist. He decided to start with the river Cam that meandered its way through the ancient university town from which it had taken its name: Cambridge. Cambridge without the Cam would be like Yale without the ivy.

Morris Fain retrieved a map from the hotel's front desk and strolled in the direction where a punt-rental landing was indicated. After hiring a boat and chauffeur, he stepped gingerly aboard. Then Fain stretched his legs lengthwise across the boat's bottom and, with his hands laced behind his head, settled in to enjoy one of the oldest pleasures offered by the city of Cambridge.

The heavy traffic on the river forced the chauffeur to do some quick maneuvering in and out of the way of oncoming punts, even as the boat left the livery dock. Fain noted with appreciation the skill with which the young man poled the flatbottom boat while balancing on a platform at the stern.

Poling was the means by which the punt gained both propulsion and direction. Punts have no oars or rudders, and most people required two or three attempts to get the hang of piloting a punt. Unwary tourists trying it for the first time sometimes were surprised to see their boat slide out from under them, leaving them suspended momentarily from their poles before the inevitable dunking.

Nobody drowns. The Cam is shallow, and there is always assistance from fellow punters, who, with gloating solicitude, will rescue any hapless gondoliers.

"I'd be happy to tell you about the sights, if you like. It goes with the punting," the strapping young chauffeur volunteered after the punt had gone a short distance with Fain as a quiet, but watchful customer. "But, if you like, I can be silent, too. What I can't do is sing."

This interrupted Fain's reverie, and he replied, "How about an abbreviated version of your tour—what we'd call the Reader's Digest version in the States?"

"I understand, sir. At times I have customers who just want to take in the sights. No talk from me. I don't mind. Sometimes it gets tiring giving the same travelogue and history lessons hour after hour. Any of the chauffeurs will tell you that."

"I don't mean to appear uninterested. Believe it or not, I really have been looking forward to this. Thing is, I'm here on some real estate business. Thinking about that's been occupying part of my mind. Nothing personal. Fact is, you handle the boat well and I'm enjoying myself. What's your name?"

"My name is Pipes, Steve Pipes."

"Where you from, Steve?"

"I live nearby in a village called Grantchester."

Morris Fain was a product of the Midwest. His college education had been of the "Big Ten" variety. Cambridge University was not only miles away from his own alma mater, it was culturally distant, as well. At the University of Minnesota, students were inputs for a giant academic enterprise whose output was thousands of homogeneous graduates. The colleges Fain observed from his punt enrolled their students by the hundreds, not the thousands. The educational process was mostly tutorial; lectures were ancillary and voluntarily attended. One judged the importance of a lecturer by the number of bicycles parked outside the lecture hall, not by the requirements of the curriculm.

On this bright early spring afternoon, everyone on the Cam and along its banks seemed to be in a festive mood. Fain took note of this as he observed people sitting along the river's edge and the other passengers in punts around him. Often he had been reminded by his friends that relaxing was not his forte.

He worked hard in the family business. It had not been easy taking over the firm from his father. He knew that many family-owned businesses failed in the second generation, and the children always shouldered the blame. If the business succeeded, second-generation owners were thought merely to have ridden the coattails of the firm's founders. If the business was unsuccessful, no one would attribute the failure to changed economic conditions.

It took a conscious effort on Fain's part to do what seemed to come naturally to everyone else: relaxing and enjoying themselves. But Fain set about making that effort.

The effort seemed to be paying off. As the punt slipped under the Silver Street bridge and approached the Backs, he found himself being lulled into a state of repose. So this is relaxation, Fain found himself thinking, as King's College came into view.

His business cares fading, Fain's eyes focused on the College's Chapel. It seemed immense against the background of its surroundings. Even at a distance, Fain could observe its majesty and splendor: the gothic spires with their intricate carvings; the heraldic emblems; the myriad of pinnacles spaced along the belfry. Fain was not usually moved by great architecture, but this was a sight he would remember.

The punt glided under Clare Bridge and around the turn past Trinity College. Pipes gave short descriptions of the various sites that were visible as he poled the way to Magdalene College, the turnaround point for the punt's journey.

Ahead, Fain spotted an impressive structure: an enclosed marble bridge that linked buildings of a college that was situated on both banks of the Cam.

"Coming up is the Bridge of Sighs named after the original in Venice, but at Cambridge it's considered the real thing. It's part of St. John's College," Pipes explained.

Fain noticed that the windows on the bridge were inset with crossing metal rods, and he inquired about them. Pipes obliged. "Those insets were put there some years after the bridge was constructed to seal off the grounds. In those days, you see, there were gate hours at all colleges, and they wanted to make sure the undergraduates couldn't sneak into St. John's after hours."

Mid-afternoon sunlight bounced off the water and brightened the flowers along the western bank of the Cam. Picnickers dotted the mown lawns. The chauffeur drew a bead on the center of the graceful arch as they glided under the Bridge of Sighs. Then he brought the punt close to the wall of St. John's College that rose from the east side of the river. Fain, reclining in the bow seat, looked back at his guide and at the scenery they had just passed. Thrushes sang on the boughs of nearby trees.

What happened next happened so fast that Fain, in his later telling of the incident, confounded important details. The first thing he could remember was hearing the ear-splitting, almost deafening crash. He remembered seeing the splinters and the punt bench lying shattered at his feet. A shiny object caught his eye, but he was too stunned to try to recognize what it was.

Steve Pipes had dropped to his knees, his left hand grabbing the side of the punt for balance, his right hand somehow maintaining its grip on the pole as he instinctively looked up the side of the wall. Still glancing upward, he rammed the pole into the water with all his strength, pushing the punt sideways—out of harm's way he hoped. He never was sure about it, but he thought he saw something move in an open third-floor window. At first it was there. Then it wasn't. Later, he wasn't sure if it had been there at all.

Chapter **4**:
Breakfast with Mrs. Saltmarsh

"Were you busy yesterday, luv?" Mrs. Saltmarsh placed a cup and saucer before her young boarder. The aromas of freshly perked coffee and hot scones filled the breakfast nook. Before he could respond, Mrs. Saltmarsh interjected, "Now try these and see if they aren't better than the scones from Taggert's. I don't know what things are coming to that a person can't get a proper scone anymore. I told Mr. Taggert that he was doing something different in the baking, but he said he wasn't, that he was doing them the same way he always had. But I know better." Mrs. Saltmarsh poured out two cups of coffee and sat down.

"Your scones are super, Mum." Steve Pipes knew which side his scones were buttered on. He had rented a room from Mrs. Saltmarsh for two years now. For three pounds a week, three hours of chores, and about two hours of appreciative listening, he got a cheerful room and a filling breakfast to start his day.

"I was busy yesterday. But not at earning any tips. My whole afternoon was spent with the police and my boss, explaining how my punt got smashed."

Mrs. Saltmarsh had started to sip her coffee, but the cup stopped halfway to her lips. "Well, I never. . . . Who smashed it, luv? Some drunken punters, if I had to guess. You take your life in your hands these days when you go out for a bit of fun. I've always thought bein' on water was dangerous enough, even when

17

people behave themselves. You're lucky you didn't get a crack in the head and a soakin' that'd be the end of you.''

Steve Pipes tossed his head back and gave a hearty laugh. ''Drunken punters I see a lot, but they're no problem. The problem yesterday was the one I never saw. Until it was over. And even then, I wasn't sure *what* had happened. All I know for certain is an iron dumbbell almost killed my customer. And because it just missed him, it almost sank my punt. Mr. Watson wasn't pleased about that, I'll tell you, but I told him it was better than being sued by the bloke's family or something.''

''How in the name of goodness could a dumbbell do that?'' Mrs. Saltmarsh's coffee cup had not moved.

''At first I thought it fell from a window in St. John's. But when I looked up, I couldn't tell. At least I wasn't sure if I saw something or not.

''I didn't have any time to think, anyway, because at first I thought it had fallen on my passenger. Almost did, too. Missed him by about two inches, no more than that. He looked as white as the top of my pole. But I looked him over, and he didn't have a scratch. We got back to the dock as quickly as we could, which wasn't easy because we were taking on water. Then Mr. Watson called the police, and I ended up having to talk to them. They sent someone up to St. John's to look around, but they couldn't find who did it.''

''I shouldn't think so,'' Mrs. Saltmarsh replied. ''Nobody wants to admit they'd let a dumbbell fall out their window. I knew a lady once, before the war, dropped a Carnival glass vase from her bedroom window. Her husband was really upset. But if you do any cleaning, you could understand putting something like *that* on a window ledge. Just for a minute, you know. But not a *dumbbell*. That's just looking for trouble, if you ask me. I'll tell you this, luv, there's two dumbbells involved here, not just one.''

Steve Pipes and Mrs. Saltmarsh sat quietly for a moment, drinking their coffee and nibbling on their scones. Mrs. Saltmarsh's other lodger had not yet come down for breakfast.

''I can tell Miss Tanner's up. I always know when I hear the water running upstairs. I hope she comes down soon because I need to go into town this morning for some fabric. There's a sale at Eaden Lilly's. I want to be there before the traffic gets too bad." Mrs. Saltmarsh paused, then started up again.

"I don't know how you could get more people into Cambridge than we've had this spring. I can hardly make my way up Sidney Street anymore with a shopping cart. I don't see how young Mums do it with their prams. Nobody gives you an inch of space. And you don't dare step off a curb, because if a bike doesn't hit you, a bus will."

"Then you need to let me take you on the river sometime," Steve replied. "It's busy, too, but not as bad as the streets."

"No thanks, luv. It sounds like it's safer in the streets. Besides, I wouldn't see any of my friends on the river. You tell me the last time you had someone from England on your boat. Not in donkey's years, I bet. Everybody who has money these days in England is either Japanese or German—or French, or they're Yanks. I asked Mrs. Diggins the other day whether England had really won the war or not."

Steve Pipes listened attentively to his landlady while he finished his first cup of coffee.

"Have another cup, luv?" she inquired of her young boarder. He nodded an assent.

Pipes enjoyed his early mornings in the small cottage near Grantchester. In a few minutes, by bicycle, he could be in the middle of Cambridge with all its amenities, but in a short time he could return to the serenities of the English countryside. Mrs. Saltmarsh's dwelling sat in a small pasture just south of Grantchester, a ninth-century farming village on the river Cam. Steve Pipes felt he had the best of both worlds.

And Pipes was not the only one who felt this way. Dolores Tanner, Mrs. Saltmarsh's newly acquired boarder, seemed pleased with the Grantchester location, its pleasantries and civilities.

"Mrs. Saltmarsh, your mattresses are just too comfortable. I overslept again. Am I too late for breakfast?"

"You just sit right down, luv, while I warm up your scones. There's plenty of coffee. And you'll have Steve to keep you company."

"Steve, you don't have to stay here on my account. If you were about to go, please feel free." Dolores Tanner seated herself at the table and began to pour milk into a steaming cup of coffee.

"I still have a few minutes. I'm not due at the river until later this morning. Besides, I'd like to hear how it went yesterday."

Dolores Tanner sipped her coffee before answering. "Okay, I suppose. It's hard to tell, really. I think it went well, but I'm not sure. Do you know what I mean?"

"Well, do you think you'll get the part? That's what I'm asking."

"I read well. I think I'm right for the part. But I'm not sure if the casting director saw that. That's what's so frustrating about this work. I get parts when I least expect them, but I don't get the parts I really want."

"What were you trying for yesterday?"

"Eve. There's going to be a revival of Shaw's *Back to Methuselah* at the Queen's. I'd die to have the part."

"If you get it, maybe I could be the serpent," Steve responded, his eyes making it clear he was kidding.

"Sorry, Steve. Wrong gender. The snake's a she. Besides, you're too late. They've already cast the serpent. I found that out yesterday at the theater."

"Here's your scones, dear, all warmed up." Mrs. Saltmarsh reentered the breakfast nook and deposited a table-basket containing two doughy pastries. "And the butter's there right in front of you. Steve, be a good boy and pass Dolores the jams."

Mrs. Saltmarsh pulled her chair to the table and proceeded to replenish her coffee. "What a lovely housecoat! What's it made of? Doesn't look like flannel. But comfy, all the same."

"Actually, it's alpaca. It may seem a bit extravagant, but in the theater, robes are public apparel. We're always meeting people in our robes. You never know who will pop into your dressing room between changes."

In the morning sunlight, the black glossy robe that had caught Mrs. Saltmarsh's attention set off the long blonde tresses of the young actress. Her hair was her best feature and she knew it. And so she spent much time cultivating it: washing it in the most delicate of shampoos; nourishing it with the latest highly touted conditioner; caressing it with brushes of the softest bristle.

Dolores Tanner also had a near-perfect complexion, a prerequisite for any young woman aspiring to the British stage. This she protected with a dozen different cleansers, astringents, lotions, and oils. On the other hand, her figure was rather plain—more of a handicap for the theatre than for the cinema.

"Well, dear, you've been with us two weeks now. Are you starting to feel at home in our little village? I know it's a far cry from London," Mrs. Saltmarsh asked, while whisking some loose crumbs from the tablecloth.

"I felt at home from the moment I got here. It's just what I was looking for. You saved my life, Mrs. Saltmarsh. Life in London was getting too complicated. I know I need to be there for my work and everything. But I know now I need to be here, too. Somewhere where I can think. In London, there was no chance for that. I was at work; and after work I was with the same people I worked with.

"Here I can walk in the fields, breathe the country air, and not have to be on display. I feel like a child again. And yet . . . yet, I'm not cut off from the city. As I was telling Steve, yesterday I had an audition in London for a part. London's only a short train ride away, but it's a world away, too.

"Of course, all that could change. I realize that. What if I got the part I auditioned for yesterday? Much as I like being with Steve and you, I'd have to leave. That's the reality of the stage. Maybe the only one."

Mrs. Saltmarsh's face took on a look of sadness at the prospect of losing her new lodger. She had been widowed during World War II; she received a small pension, but she depended upon her tenants for the additional income needed to help her maintain the home she and her husband once shared. And she also wanted the company. Preparing a breakfast for herself was a lonely task. Preparing a breakfast for her young lodgers she found to be no chore at all. "They're young; they keep me young, too," she would say to her neighbors.

Steve Pipes had his own thoughts on the subject of Dolores Tanner's prospects. He found her attractive and enjoyed being with her. To him, her life was glamorous—so different from the lives of the other girls he knew. His selfish instincts made him hope she would stay. But his better nature made him hope she would get the part.

Steve Pipes rose from his chair and placed his napkin beside his plate. His eyes looked down at the table for a moment. "If you get the part, I'll be happy for you, even if I never have the opportunity to see you in the play."

"Oh, but I'd want you to come. I could see that you got some tickets. You too, Mrs. Saltmarsh. I'd want you both there on opening night."

"That'd be fun, wouldn't it, Steve? Seeing Miss Tanner in a play, I mean. And opening night? I'd be the envy of all my friends." Mrs. Saltmarsh's face had lit up at her lodger's offer.

"If the play comes to Cambridge, sure, I'll be in the audience. We could talk after the play, perhaps. But in London you probably wouldn't have time for me."

Steve Pipes's peevish tone was a surprise to Dolores Tanner. But Mrs. Saltmarsh understood.

Chapter 5:
Balliol Croft

The trio stood together on a gravel driveway that ran to the east side of the house. The large brick house that loomed before them was a Queen Anne Revival with a catslide roof. It had, on either side, great chimney stacks tied together by arches and two symmetrically placed white-sashed dormers. Off the left front, at ground level, a midget bay window projected from the drawing room.

From his vantage point, Spearman could see the detailed timber framing of an upper floor veranda. The veranda door led into a room Spearman knew had been the study of Alfred Marshall. The sight of the house had to inspire awe in any economist brought up, as Spearman had been, in the belief that microeconomics was the core of the discipline. Marshall was the father of microeconomics.

So that's Balliol Croft, Spearman thought to himself. He had often wondered what it would look like, ever since he had read the preface to Marshall's *Principles of Economics*. Thousands of professors had ended the prefaces of their books with their home institution. Marshall had signed his preface with his home address. Spearman could see it still in his mind's eye, just the way it appeared on the page:

Balliol Croft

6 Madingley Road, Cambridge

Alfred Marshall's move from Oxford to Cambridge had been
made with considerable reluctance. The name Marshall gave his
new dwelling had helped to soften the blow of leaving his beloved
Balliol College at Oxford. It was the enclosed character of the
expansive green yard that had moved him to add the word "Croft"
to the Balliol designation.

"We're a little bit early," Henry Spearman said to his two
companions. "Do you think we should wait or go on up?"

"What time is our appointment?" Pidge replied.

"Nine A.M.," Fain responded.

"Well it's almost five to nine now. I think it's all right to let
them know we're here."

Their hesitancy was ended by a booming voice coming from
the side of the house. "If you're with the f-f-foundation, do come
on up. I've been expecting you." Duncan Thring greeted the
Spearmans and Morris Fain with a hearty wave and beckoned
them to the side door.

Thring was a lanky Englishman in his late sixties wearing a
tattersall shirt and grey woolen trousers. His friendliness caught
Fain off guard since his correspondence always had been stiff. In
person, Thring's easy smile and effusive manner made his guests
feel at ease.

There is a widely held impression that the English are a stuffy
people. This view is incorrect. They are a people of propriety.
Stuffiness is the appropriate response only when the situation requires it. But other situations generate totally different categories
of behavior. The English, more than other peoples, can make this
transition almost effortlessly. Duncan Thring knew that business
letters to strangers were supposed to be formal. But he also knew
a relaxed atmosphere should accompany amicable negotiations in
face-to-face transactions.

Walking down a narrow hallway, Thring ushered his guests into
a sitting room on the first floor. "I think we'll be c-c-c-comfort-
able here. Would you like some co-coffee before I show you the
house?"

"Coffee might be nice," Pidge replied.

"Same for me," Fain added.

"None for me," Henry remarked with a dismissive wave. He
had not yet gotten used to English coffee, which, he thought, must

be what melted cardboard would taste like. He conceded English tea was superior.

"Milk and sh-sh-sugar?" Thring asked.

Thring had a distinct stammer that punctuated his speech, but as he made small talk, it was apparent that his speech impediment caused him no embarrassment. In fact, he gave the opposite impression. The hesitancy between his words seemed natural to him, as if it were as much a part of his personality as his long white hair. After Thring left the room and made his way to the kitchen, his guests settled back and surveyed their surroundings.

Some rooms give a feeling of security that derives from their stolidness. The sitting room of Balliol Croft was such a space. The sturdy brick exterior of the house enveloped solid plaster interior walls, which themselves seemed supported and framed by the chair rail and cornice moldings. The room was spacious without seeming large. What Duncan Thring and his wife used for entertaining family and friends, Henry Spearman was envisioning as appropriate for small receptions and discussion groups.

Thring returned with two cups of coffee, some sugar, and milk on a tray, which he placed on a glass-topped table. After serving Pidge and Fain, he pulled up a wooden rocking chair.

"This is a lovely room, Mr. Thring," Pidge remarked. "It is so gracious—a feeling of having been lived in."

"Well, it has been lived in. Thirty years of ma-marriage and four children make a lot of living. And, of course, more relevant to you, the Marshalls lived here together for almost forty years and entertained p-p-people like Jowett. I would assume all the Oxford and Cambridge economists of Marshall's era sat in this room at one t-t-t-time or another.

"I su-p-p-p-p-pose I should f-feel daunted by my predecessors in this room. But fortunately for me, I'm not an economist and so I've never been w-weighted down with any intel-ell-ell-ectual legacy from the house. Hardly a week goes by without someone reminding me that someone they think is more important than I am li-lived here."

"How do they make that known?" Henry asked.

"Oh, you can't imagine. We have strangers knocking at the door and asking if they co-could see Alfred Marshall's study or his ver-ver-anda. And then some p-p-people simply walk around the house, p-peering in windows and tramping on the lawn, as if this were pu-pu-public pr-property. And then many of them want to take ph-ph-ph-photographs. Some people write le-letters to this address, as if I were not an owner, but a cu-curator. The letters come from all over. Last month there were two from Japan. M-m-my wife used to reply with a note that this was now our home, and we have no connection to Mr. or Mrs. Marshall. We've even had inquiries about Sarah, who we now know was their maid.''

"Well, when you purchased the house, did you acquire the household furnishings as well?'' Fain asked.

"No, we bought the home and the grounds, that's all.''

Fain pursued the point: "What about Marshall's personal effects? Any papers, correspondence, documents, or personal momentos? Items of that kind, even if they have no monetary value, would be of interest to my foundation. I mean is there anything left behind from Marshall's day that we might put on special display for visitors to the house?''

"I'm afraid not,'' Thring responded. "Now it's true the Marshall family did leave some things behind. My wife and I found some letters from Marshall to his mother, a rusty razor I assume belonged to him, and even some old photographs—all of which we sent straight to the Marshall Library. We didn't want to keep such things here. Oh yes, I remember, too, my wife found some clothes left by the family in the attic. As far as I remember, those went to charity.''

Thring changed his tone. "Don't misunderstand me, now,'' he went on. "Ba-Balliol Croft is no King's College Chapel, where every Cambridge tourist goes. But your m-man Ma-Marshall has his following; my family could attest to that.''

"And it's precisely because of his following that we're here.'' Spearman sat forward on the couch as he spoke. "As I suspect you've learned from some of your visitors, many consider Alfred Marshall to be the creator of much of modern economic analysis. That's why Mr. Fain's foundation wants to preserve this house, not just as a curiosity to be photographed, but as a working memorial to Marshall.''

"Well, I know your man is a grandee. I'm a Fellow at St. J-J-J-John's, and my college has a portrait of Marshall in the Hall. Not many Fellows at St. John's merit a painting, you know. The

Masters, of course, they all get pa-pa-pa-painted. There's a portrait of every Master somewhere in the College. Even the ba-ba-bad ones. But not many professors. So there's certainly something to what you say.''

Spearman noticed the effectiveness with which Duncan Thring controlled his stammer. It punctuated Thring's remarks as if to underscore selected portions of what he said. He imagined Thring was a captivating lecturer, turning a handicap into a valuable asset. Spearman was reminded of his friend, Anthony Digilio, who as a child contracted polio, which left him badly crippled. Digilio became Dean of Harvard's business school.

Once, in Spearman's presence, Digilio was asked how he could achieve such success, given his impairment. Digilio's answer surprised everyone. Far from impeding him, his illness received the credit. Having polio as a boy meant he could not play with children his own age. He was left in constant contact with adults since he could not readily play with other children. Digilio realized that if he did not make a pest of himself, most adults stood ready to assist him in whatever he tried to do. When Digilio wanted to learn about chemistry, a professional chemist volunteered to teach him. When the boy wanted to learn to swim, he was unable to bicycle to the local swimming hole, so his town's most prominent swim coach offered to instruct him. Once an art historian in a nearby city proposed to take Digilio on a tour through the galleries of Washington, D.C., merely upon learning the boy had expressed curiosity about oil painting. Spearman imagined that something similar could explain Thring's rise to intellectual prominence, in spite of his impediment.

Duncan Thring waited for Pidge Spearman and Morris Fain to finish their coffee and then announced: "I suppose it's t-t-time for the tu-tour.''

Methodically, Thring took his guests upstairs and down, outside and in the old house. He did not miss a nook or a cranny. The well-preserved cupboards and closets had not been altered since the architect, John James Stevenson, had designed the house for the Marshalls.

Thring's tour included the timbered balcony off of Marshall's upstairs study, which fronted the house and gave the structure its distinctive appearance. All of the rooms were given careful scrutiny while Thring elaborated on each part of the house.

The foursome then exited to view the home's lawn, which was bordered on all sides by tall shrubbery. Thring was especially animated when pointing out a part of the garden where Marshall, an outdoor enthusiast, worked while seated on a platform that could turn to catch the sun.

"I'm not surprised Marshall had such a contraption," Henry Spearman remarked. "He did some of his best work out-of-doors." Pidge had heard before from her husband the story of how Marshall was sitting on the roof of his hotel in Sicily while on holiday. Suddenly he hit upon an idea that became a basic economic concept. He called it 'elasticity.' Mary Paley Marshall, Alfred's wife, as well as his sometime collaborator and former student, wrote a memoir in which she reported her husband was "highly delighted with it."

"Duh-duh-delighted? Somehow that doesn't fit my impression of what the man was like. I never met him, mind you. But the pictures I've seen show him as dour and solemn, sitting there with those p-p-piercing eyes under a skullcap you might expect to see a Ch-Ch-Chinaman wear."

"You're probably right about Marshall," Henry Spearman replied. "I never heard of him being the life of the party. But the discovery of elasticity was a special occasion. Marshall must have seen its implications and couldn't help being proud of himself."

Thring feigned interest as the four began to make their way back to the house. "How would you rank the discovery of elasticity?" he inquired. "Is it the economist's equivalent of Darwin's theory of natural selection, to pick another Cambridge luminary?"

"No, nothing that monumental. The only thing we have in economics to match Darwin's theory came from an Oxford man, not a Cambridge man. Adam Smith's theory of the invisible hand is in that select category."

Spearman halted in his walk, bringing the foursome to a pause. "But make no mistake. The discovery of elasticity ranks with Crick and Watson's discovery of DNA's double helix. It enabled economists to chart movements in revenues brought about by changes in price. To give you an example, without it, your Chancellor of the Exchequer couldn't make an educated guess about how much revenue would come from a tax.''

Returning inside, the group toured the basement. The final stop was the attic, where the Spearmans quizzed Thring about the condition of the roof while Fain examined the rafters and floor boards.

After returning from the attic, Duncan Thring settled again into the rocking chair while his three American guests took the chairs they earlier had occupied. Henry rustled through some papers in his briefcase, and then stated: "It appears to me the house has been well maintained. But I'm no expert. I can barely change a lightbulb, as my long-suffering wife can attest. So I am in no position to evaluate things like the furnace and the wiring."

"Henry, I wouldn't worry too much about that. We can have those features of the house appraised by an expert," Fain interjected. "I can tell from the layout of the house that it would suit the purposes of the foundation. Your wife probably has a better eye than either of us for the condition of the house." Fain looked in her direction.

Pidge nodded to her husband and Mr. Fain. "I think the house is very sound. You can tell a lot about a place by the condition of the attic and the basement. You can cover up problems on the main floors. But not at the top and the bottom."

Morris Fain turned to his host. "I think you may have what we are looking for. The question that remains is how much my foundation would have to pay to get you to part with Balliol Croft. Of course, before any final decision is made, I want to confer with Professor Spearman and then get back to you."

"Pa-pa-parting with Balliol Croft will not be easy for me. I am attached to the house. But since my wife died last year, it has been di-di-difficult living here. So many ma-memories, you know. My children have persuaded me I should get a comfortable place somewhere near the C-College. I haven't found one yet. All in good time, I figure. But if an attractive offer comes along, I won't reject it.

"As you know from our earlier correspondence, there is another pah-pah-party seriously interested in the house—Nigel Hart, the Master at Bishop's. And I would not be honest with you if I did not tell you frankly that I'd rather keep the house in university hands. There's nothing anti-American in that, mah-mah-mind you. But I've known Ha-ha-hart for years.

"He is retiring as Ma-Master and thinks this house would be ideal for him. Of course, we haven't talked pr-pr-prices. My children tell me a price of 18,000 p-p-pounds for the property would be fair. That sounds right to me. A house down Ma-ma-madingley Road—not nearly as well maintained as this one, and without this home's pr-pr-provenance—sold recently for 16,000 p-pounds.

"Of course, I'm not an economist, but does that seem fair to you?" Thring looked at Henry Spearman, opening his hands imploringly.

"Not even Alfred Marshall could say what was a fair price for his house. But he might make a stab at the *right* price—that is, a price that would make both the seller and the buyer better off as a result of the sale."

Henry Spearman paused for a moment. "There may be quite a number of prices that meet this condition. And how it all comes out depends, to some degree, on the bargaining skills of the parties."

"I've never been much of a ba-bargainer, but I must say the price I quoted you is probably firm. I cannot imagine my bu-bu-budging very far from it," Thring replied.

"Oh, I can," answered Spearman, looking at Thring and smiling. Even Pidge looked surprised at her husband's cool confidence.

"Well I don't see how you can say that. I think I mean it when I say it's 18,000 p-pounds firm," Thring responded.

"But if I told you I was prepared to offer 19,000 pounds, how firm would your asking price be then?"

Thring at first looked puzzled, then his lips turned to a grin. "Aha, I see what you mean. Another one thousand pounds would melt away my f-f-f-firm resolve."

"Well, then, you can see our difficulty," Spearman responded, still smiling broadly at his host. "If you are so flexible upwards, how can we be confident that you are not flexible downwards, as well?"

Spearman had risen to his feet and was gesturing toward Fain with his hand. "Before we go, Morris, you must tell Dr. Thring about your close shave yesterday."

The Englishman turned to Morris Fain. "What's this about a

close shave? Don't tell me. I bah-bah-bet I can guh-guess.'' Thring became quite animated. "It happens to our American visitors all the time. Now tell me if this isn't exactly what happened. You were about to cr-cr-cross the street. So you l-l-looked to the left. You saw the way was clear. So you assumed all wa-wa-was safe. Then you stepped off the cu-curb. And at that point you were almost run down by a Cambridge bu-bu-bus coming from the other direction!'' Thring spread his hands in triumphant satisfaction. "Now is that it or not?''

"Nothing so pedestrian, if you'll pardon the pun,'' Henry Spearman responded. "You'll have to tell him what really happened, Morris.''

"I discovered yesterday afternoon that punting is not as safe as it looks.''

"How so?''

"Do you know where the corner of St. John's College rises from the Cam? Well, I had rented a punt and a chauffeur, and as we were floating past that spot, I was almost killed by a dumbbell.''

"A du-dumbbell?'' Thring asked incredulously.

"Well, yes, it was a 25-pound handweight. Of course, I had no idea what on earth it was when it first hit the punt. I was seated in the bow of the boat looking back at the chauffeur. Just before, I had been looking forward at the Bridge of Sighs. Of course, I never thought to look up. So I had just settled back and there was this terrific crash. It was a narrow miss, I can tell you that. The dumbbell totally destroyed the punt seat just ahead of me. We were lucky it didn't break through the floor of the boat and sink us. If the weight were any heavier, that would have happened. Splintered wood was everywhere.''

Fain's eyes widened as he continued the story. "I have to hand it to the chauffeur. He seemed to know instinctively the object had come from above, and he pushed us immediately away from the building. I was too stunned to think of that. But he did. Neither of us knew what had happened, but he tried to insure that it wouldn't happen again. I actually thought, at first, we had taken some kind of artillery hit. You cannot imagine the impact 25 pounds of iron can have from a height of thirty feet or so. I have no doubt that if the punt had been two feet further back, I would not be here today looking at Balliol Croft.''

"How terrible!'' Thring exclaimed. "Inexcusable. Really inexcusable! I hope you informed the pr-pr-proper authorities.''

"Oh, the chauffeur reported it, all right. He said he had to tell the police for insurance purposes.''

"I meant the c-c-college authorities—at St. John's. The undergraduates nowadays are hopelessly irresponsible. In my time, something like that would have had us sent down. Much too serious. Oh, of course we had our pr-pranks and mischief making. And those with rooms over the river sometimes dropped a bit of water or a p-p-pillow on the heads of passersby. But usually with a warning. 'Heads up!' they'd say. Of course it was too late by then, but nobody was ever hurt. All good clean fun.''

"Surely it was an accident, not a prank,'' Henry Spearman responded. "It's hard to imagine even the most mischievous students not calculating the possible consequences of dropping a dumbbell near someone's head.'' The tone of his voice made it apparent Spearman thought Thring was on the wrong track.

"But are those the only alternatives?'' Pidge's question caused everyone's head to turn in her direction.

"What else is there?'' Fain looked puzzled.

Pidge looked at him intently, but did not offer an immediate reply.

Henry, who had caught the drift of his wife's speculation, demurred. Then he said, "Unlikely.''

"What's unlikely?'' Fain inquired.

"My husband thinks the third alternative is unlikely,'' Pidge responded.

"And that is. . . .?''

"That someone deliberately attacked you.''

"Why would anyone do that?'' Fain chuckled. It was a nervous chuckle.

"Because someone might not want you to occupy Balliol Croft.''

Chapter 6:
The Humpty Dumpty Theorem

"John Harvard was a Cambridge man. Our speaker's university and this institution have a common bond. In addition to his Harvard professorship, our guest has received several honors in the field of economics. I shall mention only two: the John Bates Clark medal of the American Economic Association and a Fulbright Scholarship. He is the author of *Alternative Paths to Equilibrium* and *Pricing in the Short-Run* in addition to many other publications. He is also a columnist for *The International Review*.

"Professor Spearman's talk this afternoon is entitled 'The Future of Communism.' If we do not all find it enjoyable, I predict we shall find it provocative.

"It is my pleasure on behalf of the Economics Speakers Club to introduce Professor Henry Spearman. He has agreed to abide by our usual format: thirty minutes of lecture, followed by thirty minutes of questions."

Having offered this introduction, the student president of the club yielded the podium and sat down.

The lecture room where Spearman spoke was the Darwin Theatre at Cambridge University. The hall was jammed. Students who could not find seats stood along the back or sat in the two aisles that converged at the lectern. The far back wall of the theatre was lined with file cabinets containing University correspondence dating back one hundred years. A haze of tobacco smoke hung high in the skylight of the elliptical ceiling.

From his vantage point, Spearman looked up at semicircular rows of seats, the backs of which served as desk tops for the students in the next rung. Above the cabinets on the back wall the speaker did not see the traditional lecture room clock, but rather a large medallion of Darwin. Cantilevered from the back wall was a small balcony that had the capacity to seat approximately twenty-five people. It, too, was filled. There was the usual hubbub and chatter Spearman expected with audiences primarily made up of students—until the moderator rose to introduce him. After that, English decorum set in, and Spearman rose to address an attentive audience.

Because his hosts had not placed a riser at the lectern, only Spearman's bald pate could be seen by the part of his audience that was close to the stage.

"The title of my talk, 'The Future of Communism,' is fraught with danger. Earlier economists tried to forecast what the future would be like. William Stanley Jevons forecast that shortages of coal would make this energy source prohibitively expensive in England. David Ricardo forecast that a growing percentage of the labor force in England would be agricultural workers. Adam Smith forecast the demise of the corporate form of business organization in the face of single proprietorships. All of these economists, though titans, were mistaken.

"Jevons discounted the importance of technological changes that would introduce alternative sources of energy. Ricardo did not foresee the application of science and engineering to agriculture. Smith could not imagine the internal mechanisms of control that financial markets and legal institutions eventually would offer to large corporate enterprises.

"Each of these economists was a brilliant scholar. Yet each was wrong in his prediction.

"I certainly do not put myself in their league. And yet I am confident that my prediction, unlike theirs, will prove to be right.

"This is not because I am more learned than they were. It is not because I have more information than they had. Nor even because economics, as a science, has progressed dramatically since their day. All of these men erred through no fault of their own. They failed to see what no one can foresee: the random exogenous shocks to which all economic systems are subject.

"My prediction will be accurate irrespective of these incalculable occurrences. The future of Communism in no way can be affected by technological advance or technological retardation. It does not depend upon favorable climates or natural catastrophes. Neither does it depend upon war or peace, or even upon whether we are governed by wise or evil leaders. What matters is whether an economic system has institutions that channel human beings in directions that are productive and satisfy their own desire to, as Adam Smith put it, 'better their condition.' Because Communism does not meet this criterion, its future is bleak indeed." His preamble completed, Spearman took a long pause, looking down at the lectern, as if studying his notes before continuing. But he was not oblivious to the consequences of his introductory remarks.

Sometimes what is felt in a lecture hall is more palpable than what can be seen. In this instance, a rising tension was discernible among the listeners. It did not manifest itself in derisive behavior. It was not even reflected by fidgeting or whispering. It was best sensed by the expression on many of the faces: a look that said, "You can't be serious?"

Spearman was aware of this mood as he continued his lecture and developed his argument. He realized that Cambridge once had been the academic home of John Maynard Keynes. Today, it was the home of Ajit Chandavarkar, Olivia Hale and Nigel Hart. All of these were economists of the left who were sympathetic to widespread government planning and intervention. Some Spearman knew to be admirers of Karl Marx. Others opted for an all-encompassing but democratic welfare state.

It is not surprising that these teachers had great influence upon the students at Cambridge. The young are impressionable. Spearman's thesis that Communism could not be self-sustaining was running against the grain. Students in the audience were eager to match their mentors' teaching against the American visitor. This did not faze the exuberant speaker at the podium as he continued his lecture. He loved an argument, thrived on it.

"I see that my allotted thirty minutes are about up, so let me conclude. I know I have not presented a consensus view. But truth is not tested by a vote. The brute force of history will determine who is right and who is wrong.

"I have not made a specific forecast today, because I cannot

say precisely when Communism will collapse. But that it will
collapse I am as certain I am right as I am that I have failed
to convince at least some of you. Now, who wants to cast the
first stone?''

Spearman stepped to the side of the lectern and adopted a relaxed pose, holding a glass of water that had been provided for
him. With a steady grip, he took a long swallow and then pointed
to an upraised hand in the sixth row. It was that of Nigel Hart.

"Professor Spearman, if America believes that Communism is
going to collapse, why do you need your missiles and hydrogen
bombs in Western Europe? Assume, for the sake of argument, that
the Russians and you go to war, and they destroy you before you
destroy them. So Communism wins and capitalism loses. Where
does that leave your argument?'' Nigel Hart had put the inquiry
belligerently to Spearman. A rippling of applause followed his
question, the loudest coming from Olivia Hale seated next to him.

Spearman responded with a back-and-forth shaking of his head,
while offering a cherubic smile. "Communism cannot succeed
because it defeats the West in a war. For that matter, the collapse
of Communism does not depend upon the existence of capitalism
anywhere else in the world. If Communist societies cannot deliver
the goods and services their people want, which I believe to be
true, then military power will prove ineffective in maintaining an
unworkable system. Communism is inconsistent with all that we
know about the motivations of human action.''

Here Spearman paused, but not to take another question. Instead, he added, "There is a popular saying in my country: 'if it
ain't broke, don't fix it.' I think I have improved upon this saying
by adding a corollary: 'if it *is* broke, don't fix it, either—sometimes.' I call this the Humpty Dumpty Theorem. Here's what I
mean by the theorem.

"The problem is not that you can't put Humpty Dumpty together again. That isn't the problem at all. The problem is in the
basic structure of Humpty Dumpty himself. He should never have
been on that wall in the first place. He totters there, moving more
and more out of equilibrium with each over-correction of the central planners until he falls to pieces. Even if all the king's horses
and all the king's men, or a business corporation, or a government

bureau, or a major foundation, could put Humpty Dumpty together again, and set him back on that wall . . ."

At this juncture, Spearman stopped his response, turned his back to the audience, and simulated placing a giant egg on a high wall. Turning to face his audience again, he paused.

Then, in a stage whisper, he mouthed a single word: "Splat!"

Olivia Hale rose from her seat. "Professor Spearman, if we may put theatrics and children's stories aside, I'd like to ask a question about economics. Your entire thesis assumes capitalism is more efficient than Communism—which entails a peculiar definition of efficiency. A proper interpretation of efficiency means full capacity, production at the lowest possible cost, and the widespread distribution of goods to all consumers. But under the system we enjoy . . ."—Olivia placed delicate emphasis upon the word "enjoy" and then added, in parenthetical sarcasm—"if one can use that word . . ." Pausing to acknowledge the audience's smattering of applause, she continued, ". . . we have unused capacity of both labor and capital, high-cost production, and an unequal distribution of goods in favor of the capitalists. In a world of scarce resources, a system that generates such waste should have little survival value."

Pointing to the medallion of Charles Darwin on the back wall, Hale continued, "We are reminded here of the survival of the fittest. Doesn't economics teach the survival of the most efficient?"

Spearman shook his head vigorously from side to side. "No, no, no. I do not accept your description of a private market economy. A private market system puts resources where they are most wanted by consumers. And consumers are not all alike. What you call waste, I call the cost of variety. As long as tastes differ, differentiated products will attempt to satisfy these wants."

Hale remained standing during Spearman's response. "How enlightening. Under capitalism, the rich drive Jaguars, while the poor ride bicycles. And all because they have different tastes."

"It's either different tastes or different incomes or a combination of both," Spearman responded. "The point is that under a market system, incomes are not static. There are profits and there are losses. We can all think of examples of wealthy people who have become poor, and poor who have become wealthy."

Olivia Hale swept her arm out to the audience as she gestured, and addressed them, rather than Spearman. "Ah yes, the majestic equality under capitalism that Professor Spearman applauds is described in a poem I learned as a child. 'The rain falls alike on both the just and the unjust fella. But mostly on the just. Because the unjust has the just's umbrella.' " An expression of satisfaction came across Olivia Hale's face as students in the audience chuckled their appreciation.

Encouraged, she shot another question at Spearman. "What is your opinion on China?"

"I'll answer that question the same way I answer questions about New York. It may be a great place to visit, but I wouldn't want to live there."

"Perhaps you have no serious answers," Hale responded, "but I raise the subject of China as a serious point. Let me illustrate. Chinese women bring containers to a store and have them filled with a cold cream from a large vat. There is one formula, available to all, rich and poor alike, at a modest price. There is no advertising, no brands, no packaging gimmicks—all of which would add to costs and price the product out of reach of the poor—leaving only the rich with cosmetics for their faces.

"The same point can be made about basic clothing and basic food provisions. Central planning exploits economies of scale, so basic goods and basic services can be made cheaply and be made available to all. The future belongs to such a system, don't you agree?"

"Absolutely not. I couldn't agree with you less, Dr. Hale. Of course, if there were only one brand of cold cream, if there were no alternative, people would want what they could get. But that is altogether different from getting what they want. Where you and I differ most fundamentally is over the issue of satisfying consumer wants."

As Olivia Hale attempted to respond, Spearman turned away from her direction and interjected: "I'll take the question from the gentleman on the right." The young man was Delmore Vine.

Vine remained seated during his question, but his words could be heard throughout the theater. "There's a matter I do not understand. In what I've read about the Russian economy, statistics show their national product will surpass the national product of the United States in the not-so-distant future, as I recall. My question is: how do these statistics square with the analysis you presented today?''

Spearman nodded gravely in Vine's direction. "What you say is absolutely true. I have no doubt at all that you have seen such statistics. But I must remind you there are two kinds of statistics: the kind you look up and the kind you make up. With regard to Soviet output statistics, those that are made up are worthless. The statistics you look up are meaningless.

"Let me give you a couple of examples. Under Communism the measure of a producer's success is not profits, as is the case under capitalism. Nor is it consumer satisfaction. Such measures are considered bourgeois, capitalistic measures and therefore unacceptable. Instead, the measures of success are very different. These targets are determined by the central planners. Sometimes they use weight, sometimes number of units. If the success of the output is measured by weight the producers have an incentive to make the products too heavy. If the measure is number of units, the incentive is to make the products too small or too thin. So chandeliers pull down ceilings and roofing metal blows off in the wind. And nails are produced the size of thumb tacks. Or only one gigantic nail is produced. There are many other examples I can name, but my point is that a major problem of a planned economy is that you cannot tell whether people are being made better or worse off simply by looking at the GNP.''

When it was clear that Spearman had finished his answer, the student moderator rose from his seat and leaned across the lectern. "Ladies and Gentlemen. I shall permit one more question. We have not yet gone to the balcony. Dr. Metzger?''

Arnold Metzger, lecturer in Law at Emmanuel College, swept his hand through his full head of hair and then pulled himself forward by the balcony rail. He nervously twirled a tassel of hair around his finger. "Dr. Spearman, I am not an economist. But I find your logic persuasive. However, there is something that puzzles me. Assuming you are right in your prognostications, why are most intellectuals so sympathetic to Communism? In this country at least, a person with your views would be a *rara avis.*''

"I think I've just been called either a strange bird or a scarce rental car,'' Spearman quipped.

The appreciative laughter was like music to Spearman's ears. He knew before his talk that he would be facing a critical audience. Long ago, Spearman learned that humor was the best solvent for hostility. But humor has its dangers. To be met with a resounding silence makes matters worse. Usually his gambles paid off. Expecting an ogre, his audience discovered a pixie.

Then he looked back with a serious expression in Arnold Metzger's direction. "There is nothing surprising about what you say concerning intellectuals. The one thing you can be certain of, regarding human beings, is that they will always place their interests ahead of yours. Intellectuals are no different from other people. In a centrally directed society, someone must do the directing. Intellectuals think they will be in charge. They'll have the position and prestige that in a capitalist economy go to successful entrepreneurs. In Soviet bloc economies, for example, professors of economics who have become central planners have the best apartments in the city, dachas in the country, and chauffeured limousines. High officials have access to special shops, where imported luxury goods of all kinds are available—including, I might add, cosmetics by Helena Rubinstein and Revlon—and these imports are purchased eagerly by the central planners."

At this point, Spearman gestured toward Olivia Hale. Their eyes met. The atmosphere now had become electric. "Does anyone really believe, even for a moment, that the apparatchik bring empty containers to the store to be filled with nondescript ointment from a communal vat? I can assure you, Dr. Hale, they do not."

Chapter 7:
Cambridge Controversies

"Fasten your seat belts everyone—it's going to be a bumpy night!" Jared McDonald led the way toward the front door of Olivia and Chandler Hale's house, the Spearmans trailing behind. His tall, lanky frame gave him an ambling gait that contrasted with the Spearmans' synchronous stride.

Before reaching the door, Jared had turned back toward them and given his exaggerated impersonation of Bette Davis in *All About Eve*. McDonald's version of Bette Davis had been his attempt to bring levity to the situation. But it also contained a warning. He had been present at the afternoon lecture and seen the high-level voltage between Olivia Hale and Henry Spearman. Jared expected more of the same at the Hales' post-lecture soiree.

"You won't be the only bait in the lake this evening, Henry," Jared said. "I have been to a number of affairs like this. My colleagues' feeding habits are cannibalistic; they also like to feed on each other."

"We won't be surprised at that," Pidge Spearman interjected. "I've come to believe it goes with the turf in academic life."

"Don't worry, Jared. Most academics who come on like piranhas—usually turn out to be minnows," Henry Spearman added.

"Maybe so. But be careful you don't get caught in the jaws of one of the Great Whites that circle around the Hales' living room," Jared responded.

The three of them had walked together several blocks from where McDonald, who had given the Spearmans a lift, had parked his car. Parking close to the university was always tight. Apologizing to the Spearmans for the long trek from the car to the Hale's home, Jared pointed out Nigel Hart's vehicle parked just ahead of theirs, indicating that despite the loftiness of his rank, the Master had fared no better than they had. Although Nigel Hart was the Master of his college, his title did nothing to shorten the distance to the Hales' home on Lensfield Road.

The two-story brick house that Jared, Pidge, and Henry approached had a solid look. Three dormers on a mansard roof faced out on the street. Eggshell white trimmed the doors and window casings. A copper weather vane in the shape of a galloping horse was centered at the roof's ridge. A cobblestone circular driveway did double duty as a sidewalk to the entrance.

Before any of the threesome could knock, the front door opened and Chandler Hale greeted them. "Come in, do come in!" Hale was introduced to Mrs. Spearman by Jared McDonald as Hale led his three guests down a short hallway to the living room where the others already had gathered.

"What can I get you?" Hale looked at Mrs. Spearman first. Pidge requested a glass of dry sherry. Jared and Henry preferred gin and tonic. "I'll bring you your drinks. Meanwhile, Jared, be a good fellow and circulate around with the Spearmans, would you? Almost everyone heard our afternoon speaker, but not everyone has been introduced to the Spearmans."

As they made their way through the crowd, exchanging introductions, Pidge thought she saw a familiar face. The familiar face saw her at almost the same time, and they headed toward each other.

"I know people say this is a small world, but this really *is* a small world," Ardis Horne exclaimed, reaching back to get the attention of her consort. "Graham, look who's here. You remember the American couple from the Bentham exhibit?" Graham Carlton excused himself from a conversation and joined Pidge Spearman and his companion.

"What a pleasant surprise to see you again," he said. "Is your husband the speaker everyone is talking about? I must confess I did not really catch your surname the other day in London."

"It's Spearman, but that's all right. I'm terrible on names as well," Pidge responded. "What brings the two of you to Cambridge? Is either of you on the faculty here?"

"No, we live in London," Ardis responded. "Graham is a theatrical producer there, and I am Olivia Hale's editor at Macilvane Publishers. She and I have become friends, and Olivia often invites me to events like this. I assume you're accompanying your husband on a lecture tour?"

"Not really," Pidge replied. "At least, that's not the main thing. We've gotten involved in a project concerning some property here in Cambridge. My husband is serving as a consultant to the Fain Foundation in Chicago."

"Fain? In Chicago? Morris Fain?" asked Carlton. "I believe I've had some business dealings with him in the past."

"Oh, I see Gregory Shepherd's here," Ardis interrupted. "He's another reason I enjoy coming to Cambridge. I hope you and your husband get to meet him this evening. In fact, you should visit his bookshop in Cambridge. He's strong in history and the social sciences." Ardis Horne discreetly gestured to the far side of the living room. "If you can see the rather portly man behind the couch—that's G. Shepherd, as he's known here."

Pidge gave a cautious sideways glance across the room. She saw a thick-necked, chesty man with jowly cheeks, whom she assumed was Shepherd.

"And who is his distinguished looking friend? The man in the Nehru jacket?" Pidge asked.

"I don't know him well. He's not on the Macilvane list. I understand most of his writing is in article form. But he is one of the mainstays in economics here. His name is—ah, what is it?—it's an Indian name. I can't quite get it."

At that moment, Pidge noticed that her husband was being led by Jared McDonald to speak to the man in question. Pidge excused herself and headed in Henry's direction.

"Oh, Pidge, I want you to meet Dr. Chandavarkar." Henry Spearman extended his hand in the direction of the Indian gentleman.

"I am Ajit to everyone. But you may call me Dr. Chandavarkar if you insist," he said to Pidge with a grin.

"I suspect no one insists on that," Pidge said.

"Ajit and I were on a panel together in Rotterdam two years ago," Henry Spearman said. "Do you remember that conference, Ajit? You showed remarkable gentleness to some discussants who never really understood your paper."

"I am sure you understood my paper, Henry, but I am also sure you did not agree with it."

"It is one thing to understand a paper; it is quite another thing to agree with it. To decide whether to agree or disagree requires you first to understand what has been said. Your discussants never got over the first hurdle, and therefore failed to be effective when attempting to jump the second. That's what I had in mind."

"That's a better homily than the lecture you gave this afternoon." Olivia Hale had overheard Henry Spearman's statement about discussants as she came up behind him.

When Spearman saw her, he smiled broadly and said, "Considering the source, I'm not sure that's a compliment."

"It wasn't meant to be."

Olivia Hale was not the typical hostess who believed she must appear nicely tailored at her own social functions. This evening, for example, she was wearing an uncoordinated blouse-and-vest combination, a pair of slacks, and sandals. Her stringy, graying hair was pulled back into a bun, making her look grandmotherly. Olivia's appearance was deceptive. Her blunt squelches had, on many occasions, left heads rolling and produced a respectful attitude from anyone who may have thought females unsuitable for academic combat.

"It is obvious from your refreshingly innocent espousal of capitalism's virtues that you are unfamiliar with my proof that capitalism is a logical impossibility. I have shown that it cannot work. However, I don't blame you for that deficiency in your education. The insularity of American economists, especially at Harvard and MIT, is a professional scandal."

Spearman started to reply but was abruptly cut off by his hostess. "Hearing you defend the indefensible would be quite tiresome. Really, Professor Spearman, we heard enough of that this afternoon. Let's switch to a topic you might know something about. I didn't hear you once mention the most important factor determining whether capitalism or socialism will triumph."

Spearman maintained his smile. "What do you have in mind?" he asked.

"The rate of interest, of course."

Here Olivia Hale had moved to a topic so controversial at Cambridge that it had divided almost all of the economists there into two groups: those, like Olivia Hale, Nigel Hart and Ajit Chandavarkar—the heirs of John Maynard Keynes—who argued that the rate of interest was a monetary phenomenon; and a smaller, much embattled group, who continued to follow the teaching of Alfred Marshall and A. C. Pigou, which treated interest as a "real" phenomenon. Jared McDonald was one of these.

The vociferousness with which this dispute was carried on, the bitterness it engendered, and the rivalries it created within the faculty had enormously corrosive effects on the academic atmosphere. Decades-old friendships were torn asunder under the strain. Much time was spent on the strategy and tactics of academic politics and the marshaling of intellectual support in favor of one side or the other.

And just what was the issue that had led to such a disturbance in what was once an idyllically serene environment?

As improbable as it may seem, it was whether the price a person pays for money—the interest rate—is a result of central bank policy that decides how much money to supply, on the one hand, and the amount of money people wished to hold as cash, on the other. This is called a monetary theory of interest. It was Keynes's position.

But to Alfred Marshall, who was once Keynes's teacher at Cambridge, the rate of interest was a real phenomenon. That is, it was ultimately determined by how much income people saved and made available for lending and by how much borrowing on the part of the public took place. It was called a "real" theory because saving was a result of being thrifty, and being thrifty involved real costs: giving up the pleasures of consuming goods today and waiting to have these pleasures in the future. And also because borrowers, especially businesses, would pay for money only as much as the real, honest-to-goodness productivity of the machines they bought with that money could justify.

There was another element in the controversy: ideology. The disciples of Keynes had taken on an extreme leftist slant after the

Master's death. Although they remained Keynesian in their espousal of his theory of interest, they embraced Marxism as a solution for society's ills. If interest rates are artificial, as Keynes believed, then to Marxists the whole rentier class of investors, bankers, and capitalists becomes unnecessary, and candidates for economic extinction. Those who held such views were conveniently referred to as Marxo-Keynesians.

"And so, Professor Spearman, understanding the rate of interest is critical in determining the outcome of our debate. In your lecture this afternoon you missed the point. When interest rates approach zero, it's not so easy for a financier or a banker to make a living without working."

Olivia Hale turned sideways to Henry. Speaking over her shoulder to her diminutive guest, her parting words were, "Yes, capitalism may survive. . . . But some capitalism! A capitalism without any capitalists!"

"Precisely what I predicted," said Delmore Vine. "The knives are flashing." The Bishop's College Fellow had overheard Olivia Hale's conversation with Henry Spearman. He had enjoyed it. "Olivia just sliced Spearman paper-thin."

Vine was talking to a group of four guests huddled together near the bar. His observation provided no conversational lead anyone cared to follow, and he was soon off to join another group of guests. Delmore Vine acted as though everyone was fascinated by everything he said. It was this megalomania that caught Nigel Hart's attention and made him eager to recruit the young Fellow into his circle.

As they mingled, the Spearmans noted that, in the course of the evening, Nigel Hart and Chandler Hale never spoke. They even took care never to be positioned in the same conversational circle. But to accomplish this, their eyes had to meet often during the party.

Insiders to the economics community at Cambridge University knew that Chandler Hale tolerated Olivia Hale's long-term relationship with Nigel Hart. Triangles were not uncommon in academic life in this day and age. But in few triangles did one leg of the geometric figure have to endure the other leg's social presence in his home.

Chandler Hale had ceded largely to his wife any authority he had over appointments and promotions at Cambridge. He continued to do research on the aggregate supply function; he published occasionally with Chandavarkar; he supervised students for Jesus College; and for two terms each academic year he gave lectures on money and interest.

Students attending Chandler Hale's lectures were treated to a peculiar pedagogy. Hale would spend twenty minutes or so reviewing the material from the last time. Only then would he begin that day's lecture. But shortly into the new material, Hale was surprised to find that much of his time had elapsed. This provoked him to spend fifteen minutes telling the class what he intended to do *next* time. The result was about a ten-minute slice of solid lecture material, few students, and a paucity of bicycles parked outside Hale's lecture hall.

Later in the evening, Henry found Pidge talking to Nigel Hart. Spearman did not know Hart's work well, but he soon observed that within the confines of a cocktail party, Hart was not as aggressive as Olivia Hale. Hart told the Spearmans that he had spent a year as a postgraduate Fellow at Harvard when he was younger, and he seemed eager to talk about professors and students he had known then.

"Do bring me up to date about Ken Galbraith," he asked Spearman. "I say 'Ken' as if I know him well. I really don't. But he told me, once, to call him Ken. He must be the most famous professor at Harvard. That must drive some people mad."

"I only see Ken at faculty meetings and at a party he gives each June at graduation. So I'm afraid I am a poor source of information. There is no doubt about his fame, however. I finally read *The Affluent Society* because so many of my students were asking about it."

Spearman changed the subject and asked Hart what he was working on these days, but Hart seemed not to want to talk economic research. Spearman knew that Hart was a theorist who, like Olivia, sought to advance the Marxo-Keynesian paradigm at Cambridge. More than any other scholar, Hart believed that all vestiges of the University's Marshallian-Pigovian traditions should be shed.

Nigel Hart and Olivia Hale shared a mutual dedication to showing that capitalism could not work—in practice, which they believed evident, and in theory, which they sought to prove. Hart endeavored to accomplish this by unceasing attention to strategy and to maneuvers that entrenched leftist theories of macro-econ-mics. Hart understood that, in the world of academics, the supply of ideas is in part a function of the supply of labor inputs. He wanted "his" people in positions of power at Cambridge.

"Delmore." The voice was Olivia's from across the room where, on a white couch, she was seated next to Ajit Chanda-varkar. "Please bring that boyish face of yours over here and tell Ajit what you told me earlier about Professor Spearman's lecture."

Delmore Vine had just begun his discussion when Jared Mc-Donald approached Olivia Hale with a question. "Olivia, do you know when the party will break up? I don't want to be rude by taking the Spearmans away early, but I am responsible for getting them home for a light dinner this evening."

"Oh, it's hard to say, Jared," Olivia said, rising from the couch. "These things have a life of their own at times. But if you must leave with our American guests, Chandler and I will quite under-stand. And I do appreciate your bringing the Spearmans over. I hope it wasn't too much trouble." Olivia Hale feigned courtesy toward McDonald.

Jared McDonald was not taken in. He knew that so long as the Hale-Hart-Chandavarkar threesome controlled academic appoint-ments at Cambridge, his prospects of advancing from Reader to Professor were nil.

The shadow of the Marxo-Keynesian influence had changed Cambridge greatly. If Marshall and Pigou were to return today, Jared had once conjectured, even these titans would not be able to pass through the leftist filter and gain faculty status.

Not that there weren't adherents to neoclassical economics. There were several. Some, like McDonald himself, were scholars of distinction. But the expression 'balance of power' did not apply to the Cambridge situation. So long as Olivia Hale, Hart, and Chandavarkar and one or two others on their side politicked and voted as a bloc, Marxo-Keynesians controlled the promotions and appointments.

As they walked along Lensfield Road back in the direction of his car, Jared McDonald asked Henry what he thought of the state of economics at Cambridge.

Spearman was silent at first. Then he sighed and answered; "A bit pathetic, a bit bizarre."

Chapter 8:
Balliol Croft Lost

Morris Fain walked briskly through the entrance of the Blue Boar hotel. As he headed toward the narrow stairway leading to his floor, he heard the desk clerk call his name. "Excuse me, Mr. Fain. There's a message here for you."

The envelope had been delivered by a messenger not more than five minutes earlier. The stationery read "Balliol Croft, 6 Madingley Road." Fain recognized the scrawl as belonging to Duncan Thring. He felt apprehensive.

When Fain had left Thring yesterday, it was understood there would be one more discussion with Henry Spearman, himself, and Balliol Croft's owner. He knew there was another potential buyer for the property, Nigel Hart. But he was hopeful. Against the chance of a successful conclusion to the deal, Fain already had lined up the necessary paperwork. He and Henry Spearman were to meet with Thring again tomorrow.

Why would Thring want to contact him before that meeting? Perhaps to give him the good news that Balliol Croft could be his; that Nigel Hart had changed his mind. On the other hand, a note from Thring at this juncture could signal bad news: the whole deal might have fallen through. That would be disastrous. In spite of knowing Balliol Croft might never be his, Fain had allowed his hopes to be raised so high he had begun to think of the place as fulfilling the desires he had for it.

With reluctance, he opened the envelope. He read these words:

My dear Mr Fain,

Circumstances have so changed that our meeting tomorrow would be pointless. This morning I decided to sell B.C. to Nigel Hart. I trust you and your foundation will not be too disappointed. Let me explain.

Hart is retiring as Bishop's Master in the spring and will be leaving the Master's Lodge. As you know, I am relinquishing my university post at the same time. So the timing of the sale is perfect for me. You, of course, wanted to take immediate possession. While Dr. Hart does not have your plans for the property, his occupancy will keep B.C. in the Cambridge fraternity, which I trust you will appreciate.

Incidentally, I did turn out to be flexible on the upward end of my asking price: I got five hundred pounds more than what I first claimed was my unbudgeable position. Professor Spearman turned out to be right after all.

Yours sincerely,
Duncan Thring

Morris Fain read the message a second time, sighed, and walked to the house phone. Within seconds, Henry Spearman's voice was on the other end.

"Henry, remember what the poet said about the best laid plans of mice and men? I've just received some bad news. Thring has decided to sell the house to Nigel Hart. . . . Yes, I am disappointed. I had hoped we would have the deal wrapped up tomorrow. . . . Well, it sounds to me as though there's no point in that. His mind's made up . . . . No, I have a handwritten message from him. I just got it. You can read it yourself if you want to come down. I'm in the lobby. . . . Our next move? I think you and Pidge should go on back to Boston. . . . No, it isn't anybody's fault. I appreciate all the help you gave me on this. But it looks like Balliol Croft wasn't in the cards for me from the very beginning. Remember that punting accident? I probably should have taken it as a hint."

"Well, Pidge did suggest someone might not want you to occupy Balliol Croft." Henry Spearman kidded Fain in an attempt to cheer him up.

"You have a very prescient spouse, Henry."

Chapter 9:
The Master's Lodge

"You can't put Matthews next to Blanshard. There's too much friction there. Put him next to Butterfield, and Blanshard next to Lord Barry. And I'd say put Jillian to the right of the Bursar. Then I think we've got a workable High Table."

Nigel Hart, the Master of Bishop's College, was reviewing the seating chart for the head table with the college butler, Mr. Pinn. The college kitchen bore the responsibility for the preparation and serving of the evening's food and drink. The college steward would hear of any deficiencies in this department. The society sponsoring the dinner was responsible for the evening's entertainment. Its incoming president would receive any complaints about the program. But any awkwardness in the seating of guests would be considered Hart's fault.

Nigel Hart was an archetypal Master. He was a distinguished economist, in keeping with Cambridge University's eminence in this discipline; he was a gifted raconteur, in keeping with the institution's reputation for conversational jousting; he had made the Master's Lodge into a locus of gracious hospitality and entertainment; and—in keeping with a contemporary requirement for the post of Master—he was a successful fund-raiser.

"Will you want me to call the group from the Lodge to the Hall, Master?" Pinn inquired.

"Yes, High Table will have cocktails in the library until about

seven. If you would, come by about that time and announce dinner. Then I'd like you to lead the group to the Hall, where the
others will be waiting.''

Hart was relieved to have the seating arrangements determined.
Who sat next to whom involved a sociological calculation of great
delicacy. A college don could be as temperamental as an opera
diva when it came to the placement of one's table companions.
Hart found this duty disagreeable, but worked hard at the task. He
liked to avoid confrontations between his guests, especially if the
stress they engendered detracted from his enjoyment of a good
Chateau Margaux.

Upon completion of a disagreeable chore, Hart always repaired
to his library. He did so because he loved books. He loved everything about them—their feel, their musty smell, their appearance.
Books gave him a sense of security and comfort that nothing else
could bestow. And when he was fortified with a glass of port and
a fine cigar, his sanctuary was where he would prefer to be above
anywhere else.

The library of the Master's Lodge at Bishop's College com-
prised the new east wing of the house, added in the late seven-
teenth century. It was classical in style, with oak shelving from
America. The bookcases on the south and west walls were fully
fourteen feet in height and the upper shelves were reached by a
teak ladder that ran on rails notched into the top of the cabinet.

Portraits of past Masters were displayed on the east wall of the
library. It was expected for the current Master to be able to recite
the biographies of each of his predecessors. This task became
more difficult as the centuries went by.

Before he became Master, Hart was an especially discriminating
book collector. He had amassed many copies of seventeenth-and
eighteenth-century economics tracts. But the pride of his assembly
was some five hundred signed, first-edition presentation copies of
the works of Oxbridge economists of the last two centuries. These
were the choice assets in a general library Hart had of several
hundred other volumes (some held for professional purposes, some
for personal pleasure) that filled the shelves of the Lodge's library.

Since assuming the duties of Master five years ago, Hart's devo-
tion to his collection had waned, necessarily. He had added very
few tracts; he did try to maintain the complete inventory of presen-

tation copies. But there was less time to read the catalogs of the antiquarian booksellers, and practically no time to browse the shelves of second-hand book stores. His secretary now filed the new additions, a task he once took pride in doing himself.

There was one book in particular Hart wished to examine tonight. It contained material that could prove useful for the evening's discussion. He walked diagonally across the room and gripped the side rails of the ladder. Noiselessly, he wheeled it to the appropriate location and climbed deliberately to the top rung. He knew right where it was. Almost without looking, his hand reached for the desired volume. He glanced at the name of its author. Jeremy Bentham.

Perched precariously on the ladder, Hart leafed through the book's pages until he stopped at a familiar passage. He read the words silently: "Nature has placed mankind under the governance of two masters, pain and pleasure."

"If Spearman was right in his lecture, one could conclude that even had Hitler won the war, life in England would not be all that different eventually." Malcolm Dallenbach, the young mathematician at Bishop's, took a sip from his glass. The cocktail party at the Master's Lodge was under way.

Mrs. Jerome Abrams, wife of the Senior Fellow in Anatomy, looked incredulous. "You can't be serious," she said.

"But I am, Martha," he replied. "You heard his lecture. I saw you there. It's really the inevitable implication of his argument.

"Look at it this way. He was saying the Soviet empire eventually will fall apart, maybe even before our eyes. If Hitler had captured England, the same thing would have happened to the Nazis. After all, their economy had lots of central direction. Nazi means National Socialist, remember? So ultimately, life in England would end up being about the same."

"And how would it be about the same for the Jews?" Mrs. Abrams asked, still with the same look of incredulity.

"Well, that is problematic," Dallenbach conceded. He paused in thought, then continued. "But we mustn't let that divert attention from Spearman's main point: centrally planned régimes can't last all that long, so wars to fight them may be premature. Olivia Hale should have appreciated that aspect of Spearman's argument.

I take the American really to be saying that the Cold War is totally unnecessary.'' Dallenbach seemed pleased to have regained ground in his debate.

But Martha Abrams would have none of it. ''Russian regimes might not last long, but the Russians are bunglers compared to the Germans. The Germans run a very different kind of ship. They could control Holland, France, and England, all from Berlin, for a very long time. Malcolm, you'd be goose-stepping around today if it hadn't been for the war.'' Martha Abrams disdainfully swept away from the bar, leaving Dallenbach pulling on his lower lip, wondering where his logic had jumped the track.

Elsewhere the guests at the Master's Lodge were more amiably disposed. Most of them were members of the Bentham Society, which would be dining at the Hall after the Master's party. But Nigel Hart had used the occasion to fulfill some of his magisterial obligations by inviting a few guests who were not associated with the Society. Dallenbach was one of them.

Fellows of Cambridge colleges generally kept track of how often they and their colleagues were invited to Lodge functions. Hart recalled from his own days, as a new Cambridge don, how sensitive he was to the tally. Now he tried to be generous to the younger academics in Bishop's.

G. Shepherd was enjoying the hospitality of the Lodge, though he was not a Fellow at Bishop's nor a member of the Bentham Society. Moreover, Nigel Hart was not obligated to Shepherd in any way socially. Hart had invited him because he liked Shepherd's company and because they both had been members of the same elite society during their student days at Cambridge. In addition, Hart admired Shepherd's knowledge of books and enjoyed talking with him about them.

G. Shepherd owned Cambridge's most prominent antiquarian bookshop and some of Hart's most prized possessions had come from the shelves of his establishment. Often Shepherd had called Hart first to inform him of a newly acquired item that would dovetail nicely with the Master's collection. And occasionally Hart would ring Shepherd to get his counsel on the advisability of purchasing a volume that was being offered to him by another source.

''I see you acquired a clean copy of Pigou's *Economics of*

Welfare. I haven't seen one in a while. Where'd you get it?''
Shepherd and Hart had been strolling together down the east wall
of the library when the book dealer noticed the newly acquired
Pigou in Hart's collection.

"It's only a reprint of the first edition, but I thought I would
pick it up. You'll never guess where I got it.''

"In an attic somewhere?''

"Actually, it was found in a punt.''

"In a punt?'' Shepherd thought his friend might be pulling
his leg.

"I didn't find it, actually. But a young man who chauffeurs
punts knew I collected economics books and offered it to me.
Somebody had left it in his boat one day and never came back
for it. He offered it to me for ten pounds.''

"I'd say you made a good buy. I'd have made you pay fifteen
pounds minimum for it,'' Shepherd twitted his host.

The twenty or so guests continued their conversation as Mr.
Pinn circulated among the group, offering fresh drinks and cana-
pés. Hart left Shepherd examining the Pigou volume and began
conversing with others with whom he had not yet interacted.

Olivia Hale's entrance was tardy, but not subdued. "Nigel,
Nigel, my dear, you see we made it after all.'' There are some
voices that carry across an entire room even at normal decibel
levels. Olivia Hale's was such a voice.

Nigel Hart strode to the library entrance where his guests
awaited him. "Good evening, Olivia. How are you? Nice to see
you, Chandler,'' Hart said with ceremonial politeness. "Do come
in. There's still time to have a drink and mingle.''

Although Olivia Hale's husband outranked her on the Cambridge faculty, this was a function of the institution's misogyny.
While each had established an international reputation, Olivia's
star had eclipsed her husband's soon after they were married. The
marriage was the subject of much discussion and conjecture in
Cambridge. Olivia had been a beautiful young woman at the time
of her betrothal to Chandler and she had attracted many suitors
before accepting Chandler's proposal. Her looks and brilliance,
combined with her growing prominence as a scholar in the male-
dominated field of economics, gave her an early celebrity that
attracted many young men to her, even after her marriage. Olivia

did little to dissuade those who courted her. Soon she and her husband had a marriage in name only.

The Hales continued to live together, regularly socialized, but increasingly went their separate ways.

Early in Olivia Hale's career, she and Nigel Hart had been brought together in the pursuit of a solution to the enigma of short-run movements in the business cycle. This work absorbed their time and attention. Even on hiking excursions in the Cotswolds, they debated the theoretical foundations of economic fluctuations. It was a topic of little interest to her husband, whose own research diverged from Olivia's.

Olivia lifted a glass of champagne from the salver extended to her by Mr. Pinn. She looked around the room and, spotting young Dallenbach, made a beeline in his direction, leaving her husband and the Master in uneasy communion.

He looked taller than he really was. The porter's uniform of black suit, black tie, white shirt and bowler added a visual three inches to Warren Thorne's short, wiry frame that had become slightly stooped in the last two years. His gray curly hair was almost white. And the glasses that he wore were now noticeably thick. But his mind had lost none of the attentiveness to detail for which Cambridge porters were known.

Warren Thorne, senior porter of Bishop's College, was strictly business today. And the students could tell it. He knew every student by name, often from the day of their matriculation. He typically greeted them personally when they came by the Lodge to pick up mail or messages.

The Porter's Lodge served as the gateway to Bishop's College and as a focal point for students who wanted to meet up with one another. Cases of homesickness also could be cured by a college porter in the role of Dutch uncle. For many students, the gray gargoyles and spires of Bishop's College did not automatically replace the more familiar trappings of a British home. Thorne was particularly adept at befriending students who felt a bit lost in the formidable surroundings of the prestigious institution.

Not many years ago, Thorne and his staff had very different responsibilities. In a world when Bishop's was *in loco parentis*, the porters were the keepers of the College curfew. Entering the

College after 11 P.M. meant scaling its walls. Entertaining members of the opposite sex in one's rooms had to be carried out without the staff's knowledge.

Those days were over. Now, Warren Thorne worried more about the behavior of tourists than that of students. A porter at a Cambridge college was no longer a moral guardian. But he needed a remarkable portfolio of personal attributes.

Warren Thorne's job description might read in part as follows:

> Wanted: Personable, observant, but discreet individual of high character to serve as greeter and gatekeeper of Cambridge University college. Must be able to relate to university students and tourists of all ages from every corner of the globe. A partial list of official duties would include: sorting and putting up of college mail; message taking for students and Fellows of the College; parcel reception; posting of forms and notices; traffic surveillance through the college gate; and serving as gendarme for the college grounds. Unofficial duties would include: curing homesickness; counseling on matters of the heart; advising on general rules of etiquette; telling stories of college history, lore and legends; and acquiring inside information on who's who and what's what at Bishop's college.

"You seem a bit tense today, Thorne," Tom Pickett remarked to his superior. An assistant porter for two years, Pickett was now well aware of Thorne's moods.

"Sundays and Mondays used to be quiet days. At one time you could slow down a bit then. But not anymore. There's no letup with the tourists these days. Today, it's the school kids from France. Tomorrow, it'll be the Italians. The students who live in G are dousing the punters again. I got reports of three bikes stolen last night. Jennings has reported in sick for the night shift, and the Master says we're to have everything shipshape for the big do this evening." The senior porter was not usually a complainer. After thirty years, Warren Thorne was no longer imperturbable.

Warren Thorne left the Porter's Lodge and strode down the brick walkway that led to the Master's residence. He had been told to inform Hart as soon as the large crate arrived from London.

It had been delayed in transit, and Thorne knew the Master had been concerned the shipment might arrive too late for the start of the dinner. The Master would be relieved to hear that the lorry from London was at the gate.

Thorne could hear the din of voices as he made his way through the Lodge's entranceway. "It's arrived, Pinn," the senior porter said, spotting the butler. "The lorry's arrived at last."

"Go in and tell him yourself. He'll be glad to hear it," Pinn replied.

"You're sure it's alright?"

"Certainly."

When Thorne entered the library, he saw that Hart had gathered most of the guests around him at the south end of the room. He seemed to be offering some kind of demonstration. Thorne edged closer but kept his distance.

Nigel Hart was showing off one of the volumes from his collection. His guests had varying levels of interest.

". . . Marshall apparently signed very few copies of his *Principles*. But this one has his signature. Isn't it wonderful? Mint condition and superb provenance. Some of you know Pigou's oft-repeated claim about this book: 'It's all in Marshall.' Pigou really believed any problem that came up in economics could be found discussed in Marshall's *Principles*. 'It's all in Marshall'—that's what he'd tell everyone over and over again."

Any obeisance to Marshall around Cambridge was greatly disapproved by Olivia Hale, even if the source was Nigel Hart. She never passed up an opportunity to demean hero worshipping.

"Oh, it's *all* in Marshall, alright," she snorted. "Everything that's trivial. Go to Marshall if you want to learn why you pay only six pence for a cup of tea but more than a shilling for a pint of beer. As if that's what economics should be all about. But don't go to Marshall to learn about the plight of the poor. The man had no sense of proportion of what's really important. Marshall didn't know wheat from straw."

"Your example is self-defeating, Olivia. Wheat from straw he did know." Jared McDonald had taken the book from Hart and was thumbing through it. It took him less than a minute of search. "Here's what I was looking for. Listen to this. 'Consider the case of joint products; i.e. of things which cannot easily be produced separately; but are joined in a common origin, and may therefore be said to have a joint supply, such as wheat and straw.' ''

"Thank you, Jared. You just made my point," Olivia Hale replied with sarcasm. "Marshall goes on and on about wheat and straw. But who gives a damn?"

"You would if you were poor," McDonald responded. Everyone knew it took courage to challenge Olivia Hale, so McDonald's colloquy had caught the attention of the group. "An increase in the demand for straw would reduce the price of flour, and that would reduce the price of bread." McDonald enunciated each word as if speaking to a slow student. "If bread's all you can afford to eat, you'd *better* care about the demand for straw." McDonald closed the book with a snap, placed the copy of Marshall's *Principles* in Olivia Hale's hand, and headed in the direction of the evening's guest speaker, who recently had just entered the room.

Warren Thorne passed by McDonald as the porter discreetly edged his way through the circle of guests and whispered to the Master, "The crate from London has arrived, sir."

"Ahh, good news. Just follow the procedures we used last year, Thorne." Nigel Hart turned to address his guests.

"Friends of the Jeremy Bentham Society, I'm pleased to announce that we can proceed to the theatre and join the others for the annual Bentham lecture, after which we shall go to the Hall for dinner. I've asked Dallenbach to escort you to the lecture. I shall be joining you shortly."

Chapter 10:
The Bentham Society Dines

"Is the speaker finished yet?" A tardy Benthamite who had driven from Oxford and just arrived made this inquiry of Olivia Hale, who was standing outside the theatre doors having a smoke.

"Oh, she *finished* a long time ago. But she's still talking!"

The Oxonian frowned uncertainly at Hale and opened the door a crack to peer in. He inched his way into the shadows and took a rear seat. Due to his tardiness, about all he heard was: "And so we can see, once again, that it is still useful to go back to Bentham to help steer us along the right path."

There was polite applause.

"Well, what did you think of that, Arnold?" Two members of the Bentham Society were walking with the others toward the dining hall for the evening's banquet.

"Certainly not as good as last year's. In any event, she had one salient point."

"What was that?"

"When she argued that a person cannot achieve pleasure from a task, in the Bentham sense, without at the same time suffering pain in its accomplishment. She claimed Bentham's two masters of pleasure and pain are not the polar opposites they are sometimes interpreted to be. I take her to be saying that one is a necessary condition for the other—that a person can't really take satisfaction

63

from a job well done unless the job has been unpleasant to accomplish. I think there is a lot of truth to that.''

Arnold walked along, composing an example in his mind that would illustrate the point. Turning his head, he continued, ''Who would be proud of writing a book if the book wrote itself?'' Satisfied he had confirmed the point, Metzger walked on, with his hands behind his back, his eyes focused on the brick walkway in front of him.

''Rubbish, absolute rubbish.'' Delmore Vine would have none of it. ''I suppose next you'll be telling me they should reintroduce caning into public schools so that students will enjoy their education more.''

''Might not be a bad idea at that,'' Metzger responded.

''Oh, is that what you think?'' Vine asked, a look of astonishment on his face. ''I can see it now.'' Vine became animated, swinging his forearm. '' 'Whack, whack, whack, take that you little brat.' 'Oh, thank you sir, you've made learning the alphabet such fun.' ''

Vine was a talented mimic. The pleasure Arnold derived from this particular demonstration almost compensated him for the pain of being bested in the argument.

The Hall at Bishop's had been set up for what the staff called a medium dinner: ten pieces of silver at each plate. A heavy dinner was fourteen; light was seven. The fifty-five place settings for the meeting of the Bentham Society meant about half the Hall was occupied, giving the staff plenty of space to maneuver.

Fellows' High Table served as the head table for the evening's dinner. Several of the guests at Hart's cocktail party were to be seated there. In addition to the Master, these consisted of the past and present officers of the Bentham Society, the evening's speaker, and their guests. The High Table was moved slightly to the side to allow for the large covered object that would later be moved into position just to the right of the table.

''Ah, the menu. Let's see what pleasures we're in for this evening.'' G. Shepherd opened the bill of fare, which he found by his place card on the table. He scanned its contents with interest and approval. Nice. Very nice, he thought. He turned to the dinner partner on his left. ''I see we're going to be served a Pouilly Fumé with our first course. That's an excellent selection, you know: dry, but with a fruity bouquet."

"I'll have to rely on your expertise for that. I really don't know wines that well," Dr. Abrams remarked.

Dina Dewhurst, a Reader in History at Newnham, was seated on Dr. Abrams' left. As she examined the menu she muttered, as much to herself as to Abrams, "The reputation the French have for cooking is really due to their language. We simply can't match it with the words available in English.

"I mean look at tonight's entrees," she continued. " 'Terrine de Caille aux Asperges'. It sounds so much more elegant in the French. We would call it asparagus soup.

"If my mother had announced to my father that dinner tonight would consist of 'Paupiette de Sole Florentine,' but she ended up serving fish and spinach instead, my father would have thought she was a practical joker.

" 'Sorbet aux Céleri et Cerfeuil.' What a way the French have of announcing celery sherbet!

" 'Filet de Boeuf á la Benjamin.' Humm. What would that be in English? We'd say beef with some vegetables.

"And then we have '*Meringue aux Fruits*.' How divine that sounds! And in print, it reads so well. But what it means, of course, is at some point in the meal we'll all be served *fruit cocktail*.

"In French, it's 'canapé.' The language has such imagination. What rhythm in just a single word! In English, it's cheese and biscuits.

" 'Sherry Trifle.' How elegant it sounds! But don't get your hopes up. That's fruit pudding.

" 'Petits Fours; Café'. Now here we have the French at their best. But who are we kidding? At the end of the meal, we'll all get coffee and some sweets," Dewhurst muttered.

However whetted the appetites of the guests might have been, the serving of the meal was being held up. It would be improper to begin without the Master.

"Has anybody seen him?" The president of the Bentham Society asked this of everyone at the head table where the Master's chair stood unoccupied.

"Not since the cocktail party. I'm not sure he even came to my lecture," the evening's guest speaker replied.

"Somebody check with the butler or the kitchen staff," the society's president directed. "I would like to get the dinner under way. Some of the members have considerable distances to travel later this evening."

One of the waiters was directed to go back to the Lodge to check on the Master. He returned with the news that Nigel Hart was not there. Mr. Pinn reported he thought the Master had, in fact, left the Master's Lodge for the dinner. No one at the Porter's Lodge knew of Hart's whereabouts.

"Regrettably, we'll just have to start without him," the president finally decided. "Everyone is seated, and it's time to wheel ol' Jeremy out."

The Jeremy Bentham Society at Cambridge University, which had been organized by the friends and disciples of the philosopher, had arranged, in keeping with the explicit instructions in Bentham's will, for the Auto-Icon always to be present at its annual banquet. This was the relevant provision in Bentham's will:

If it should so happen that my personal friends and other Disciples should be disposed to meet together on some day or days of the year for the purpose of commemorating the Founder of the greatest happiness system of morals and legislation my executor will cause to be conveyed to the room in which they meet the said Box or case with the contents there to be stationed in such part of room as to the assembled company shall seem meet.

University College was pleased to cooperate with Cambridge University and each year permitted the transport of the sizable mahogany case containing Bentham's body.

The president of the Society called the gathering to order and took the corner of the tarp covering the glass-faced box that contained the Auto-Icon. "Members and friends of the Jeremy Bentham Society, many years ago our founder went to great pains to give you the pleasure of his company this evening."

There was an undercurrent of chuckling at the pun as the tarp was slowly drawn aside.

At first there was silence.

Then a gasp.

Then a scream.

Delmore Vine fainted.

Slumped in Jeremy Bentham's chair was Nigel Hart. A trickle of blood marked the corner of his mouth. From under the large straw hat, his eyes stared vacantly.

Chapter 11:
A Deadly Indifference

Summer rains had turned the lawns of the homes on Appleton Street in Cambridge, Massachusetts, a bucolic green. The smell of newly mown grass came through the front windows of the Spearmans' Victorian dwelling. From a radio in the kitchen, Steve and Eydie could be heard singing their recent hit:

You're lunching at 21 and watching your diet.
Declining a charlotte russe, accepting a fig.
When out of a clear blue sky, it's suddenly gal and guy.
And this could be the start of something big.

"I think I'd take the charlotte russe. But then, the songwriter doesn't tell us the relative prices." Henry Spearman had just entered the back door. "Maybe I should use those two commodities as examples in my theory class. My students are probably tired of apples and oranges."

"Henry, your students wouldn't know what a charlotte russe is, and I doubt if many of them ever have seen a fresh fig. Just the dried-up variety. You'd better stick with apples and oranges."

"Are you calling my students culinary illiterates?"

"No, it's a lack of exposure. They don't dine in places like Club 21. They eat at the Oxford Grill. If they don't care about their weight, they have a banana split. Otherwise they have a fruit cocktail. But try working those into a song."

"That's not impossible, dear. Let me think." Spearman put his hand to his chin and closed his eyes. Then he opened them.

"How's this?" He began to sing off-key:

"You're at a luncheonette and watching your diet.
Accepting a bowl of fruit declining a split.
When out of the clear blue sky,
It's suddenly girl and guy.
This could be the start of a perfect fit."

Pidge chuckled at her husband's improvised lyrics. "Henry, maybe you can drop apples and oranges and go with your dessert examples. But for your students' sake, stick with lecturing. *Don't* switch to singing."

"You're right, Pidge, because the song doesn't permit me to make the point."

"The point being?"

"The point being there's bound to be combinations of banana splits and fruit cocktails between which my students would be indifferent. They'd just as soon have one as the other. Rejecting a sundae and accepting a bowl of fruit is a profound act in what Marshall called 'the ordinary business of life.' A person who can do that has solved the riddle of choice. How does one overcome indifference and make a choice, after all? It's not so easy to explain theoretically."

Spearman paused a moment, then tried. "Every combination of quantities of any two goods can bring as much happiness as some other mixture of these goods. So showing how somebody chooses between them, when he's otherwise indifferent, is one of the great insights economics has to offer."

"Well I hope you don't mind," Pidge said, with a design to ending the lesson, "that there's only one choice for dessert tonight: Boston cream pie."

"I'm never indifferent to that."

Dinner in the Spearman dining room was usually a pleasant experience. Like most happily married couples, the Spearmans used this time to show their interest in the other's activities of that day and those planned for the morrow. But lately this pleasure was tempered by the clutter of ladders, tarps, a table saw, and paint cans.

After a dozen years of occupancy in a house that dated back two generations, the Spearmans had decided some remodeling was in order. A new roof, the addition of a front porch, and the renovation of the bathrooms were under way.

"I need to ask you something," Pidge said, while passing horse-radish sauce to her husband. Henry enjoyed this condiment with corned beef and cabbage. "The contractor told me today there's room for two sinks in our bathroom only if we don't put in a separate shower stall. If we have the shower head over the bathtub, then we can have separate sinks. What do you think we should do?"

"You say the choice is between one sink and a shower stall or else we each can have a sink and no separate shower—is that the tradeoff?"

"That's what Mr. Duncan told me. He's gone over the plans carefully, he said."

"I'm not sure which I'd rather have," Henry responded. "How do you feel about it?"

"Well, I think I'm indifferent, too."

"Did he give you an estimate on each possibility?"

"He did, and I wrote it down somewhere, but I can't remember right now which one cost less."

The ringing of the phone interrupted the Spearmans' discussion.

"I'll get it, Henry. I think it is for me." Pidge went to the kitchen and picked up the receiver of their extension phone. "Henry, I was mistaken. The call's for you. I think it's long distance."

Henry rose from the table, left the dining room, and took the phone from his wife.

"Hello. . . . Yes, yes, this is he." Spearman listened intently to the caller.

"What? . . . When? . . . Incredible! . . . Surely that's just a coincidence. I wouldn't be worried at all about that if I were you. . . . Well, let me talk to Pidge and we'll see when we can leave. . . . Give me a number where you can be reached. Are you still at the Blue Boar? . . . You've moved to the Arbor House? O.K. I'll call you there as soon as I can arrange things over here." The receiver went back in the cradle.

"What's wrong, Henry?"

"That was Morris Fain. He wants us to come back to Cambridge. Balliol Croft is on the market again. Nigel Hart has been found dead. Murdered. I'm afraid that someone was not indifferent as to whether Nigel Hart lived or died."

Chapter 12:
The Apostles

Logan to Heathrow. The Underground to King's Cross. And then the train to Cambridge. Jared McDonald met the Spearmans at the station and drove them directly to his home. Henry and Pidge had taken one day to rearrange their plans following Fain's unexpected phone call.

That evening they boarded a transatlantic flight, which brought them into London at 6:30 the next morning. Clearing customs at Heathrow was a slow process; the officials seemed determined to open every third suitcase. But there were no bottlenecks on the tube and no wait for the next express train to Cambridge. By ten o'clock, the Spearmans, exhausted from a night's travel, found themselves in Jared's sitting room.

Jared McDonald lived in a small brick house in the area north of Victoria Road, about a half mile from Jesus Green, the grassy field contiguous to Jesus College. His abode was less spacious than the homes of many of the Cambridge dons with his years of service. But McDonald, who had no independent means, was a bachelor, and he had found this dwelling more than adequate for his personal needs and social obligations.

"No, no, I insist the two of you stay right here. It was bad enough last time my having to share you with a hotel. There's plenty of room here and I shall leave you undisturbed while you are on assignment. The last time you were here the three of us

73

hardly saw each other, except during that merry evening at the Hales. And besides, the rates are better here than at the Blue Boar.''

Jared McDonald had made a convincing case. Indeed, the Spearmans were relieved by his importuning. Pidge welcomed the informality of a home; Henry welcomed the good fortune of having a confidant close at hand.

"It's settled, then. Let me take your luggage and show you your room.'' McDonald led the Spearmans to the east corner of his house, where there was a small guest room just down the hall from the first-floor bath. It was furnished in quiet good taste. There was a floor lamp just inside the door. Twin beds were separated by a walnut night stand, which supported a small reading lamp. A window, bordered by floral-patterned draw draperies, allowed the morning sun to brighten the room. A small desk with a backless bench sat opposite the beds. Jared McDonald pointed out, "My bedroom's upstairs, so I won't be in your way.

"Now, I realize you're both exhausted," McDonald continued. "Whenever I fly back from America, I'm absolutely drained. So if you want to take a nap for a couple of hours, I'd understand. On the other hand, if you want to hear the grisly details now, I'm not teaching until this afternoon. It's up to you.''

Henry Spearman responded: "Curiosity may kill the cat, but it simply keeps me awake. So there's no point in my attempting to take a nap right now. I'd never get to sleep.''

Pidge joined in: "Jared, I can sleep anywhere, including on a plane. So I feel rested and all ears.''

McDonald led his guests back to the sitting room and seated them on a chesterfield sofa. The room's ambience had just enough untidiness to make it livable. The sofa faced a brick fireplace with an arched hearth. Centered on the mantel was an inlaid bracket clock. On the wall above the clock hung an excellent reproduction of Renoir's *Luncheon of the Boating Party*.

Jared McDonald sat down and began to recount the circumstances surrounding the murder of Nigel Hart. He explained that although he was not a member of the Bentham Society, he did receive an invitation to Bishop's Hall for the Society's now infamous dinner. And like every member of the Cambridge academic community, Jared had heard all the gruesome details over and again.

At lunch, at High Table, at morning coffee, and afternoon tea, no one was interested in anything else. However, what astonished the Spearmans was hearing about the mahogany case in which the victim appeared.

"That's an amazing coincidence," Pidge exclaimed. "Henry and I had just seen the Bentham display in London on our last visit. Less than two weeks ago. You mean someone killed Nigel Hart and put him in the case with Bentham?"

"Not exactly, Pidge. The way the police figure it, Hart was stabbed while the box was in the storage area off the College's kitchen. The police never found the murder weapon."

"So where was Bentham?" Pidge inquired.

"I'm afraid not in a position to inspire anyone. The killer had pulled the body out of the case and stashed it. Old Jeremy was found in the maintenance closet of the garage."

It took a few moments for the Spearmans to absorb this last tidbit. Finally Henry asked Jared, "Do the police have any leads?"

"That's the most astonishing part—at least to me. Can you believe that *I'm* a suspect?"

"Why you?"

"Why me? That's what I keep asking. As you know, Hart and I were on opposing sides in recent political battles within the economics faculty. So the police, in a desperate search for suspects, have latched onto the idea that academic feuding was a likely motive. Of course, I can understand how outsiders might think that. At the Hales' cocktail party, you saw for yourselves how nasty we can all be to each other. But murderous urges are one thing. Their execution is quite another."

"Are you the only suspect? How about the rest of your colleagues who share your views about the direction the Department should take? Aren't they just as likely to want Hart out of the picture?" Spearman asked the question as much to elicit information as to comfort his friend.

"The police are questioning them, too. But they seem to have settled mostly on me. Maybe it's my tongue. Maybe it's because I'm the most senior and they think I have the most to gain. I've even wondered if it's because of the letter I wrote—it must have been four years ago—that was critical of the local police department for the way it was treating the problem of vandalism at the University. They say the police have thin skins and long memories. I really don't know for sure about any of these. They are all conjectures on my part."

"I know economists at Cambridge have been deeply divided. You and I have talked about that in the past. I can understand how killing Hart might satisfy someone's vindictiveness. But it wouldn't accomplish anything beyond that, would it?" Henry inquired.

"That's the ironic thing, Henry," Jared responded. "For the first time, one could make a case that it wouldn't. A few years ago—indeed just a couple of years ago—I could see that happening. The Marxo-Keynesians now are so strong numerically that Hart's death really doesn't hurt them. Politically, I mean. Especially since Chandavarkar joined them. He is always a faithful ally. With Hart's death, I'd size up the balance of power as being unchanged. Surprising as it is to realize, they are still in control. Hart's death does nothing to diminish the chances of determining the next senior appointment by Olivia Hale and her clique."

"Well, then, it doesn't matter whether or not you go to jail," Henry kidded his friend. "The future of economics at Cambridge is not at stake. What have you told the police?"

"Well, I haven't apologized for the letter, if that's what you mean. At least not yet. But I have tried to explain to them that disputes among professors have been going on here for years— even among the titans. I even told them about the Apostles."

"The Apostles?" Pidge wondered out loud.

"The Apostles, Pidge, is an exclusive club of intellectual elitists here at Cambridge." Henry Spearman was responding to his wife. "Keynes was a member, but by no means the only distinguished one. You'll have to help me with some of the other names, Jared."

"E.M. Forster, Frank Ramsey, G.E. Moore, Lytton Strachey, Ludwig Wittgenstein, Bertrand Russell. Those were some of them. My point to the police was that the group was full of intrigue and jealousies. But they didn't kill each other. Actually, it was more a matter of people dying to get in.

"I can remember an incident, years ago, when a young Fellow from Trinity by the name of Hesketh—a rather promising economist, I thought—took his own life after he was blackballed from the Apostles. Hesketh actually was in very good company. Years earlier, Keynes had blackballed Pigou simply because Keynes wanted to be the only economist in 'The Society.' Rumor had it that Hart did the dirty work on Hesketh, though Keynes may have been the inspiration.''

"What a tragedy! He killed himself just because he didn't get in?'' Pidge asked in reaction.

"It was an even greater tragedy than you imagine. He left behind a wife and 10-year-old daughter. I was told the mother was left unbalanced by the event, and the little girl was raised in various foster homes.''

Jared reflected, then turned to Henry. "Oddly enough, I remember the little girl in an incident that involves Balliol Croft. I was there once when she was with her father. Mrs. Marshall let her play with some colorful stock certificates that her husband had brought back from America. Not many people know that Marshall visited America before he was married. I once read some of the letters he sent home—must have been something of a momma's boy. Wrote her a letter most every day. I remember in one of them he reported there was 'scarcely a virtuous woman in the state of Nevada.' At the time, I wondered how he learned that. In any event, the little Hesketh girl was fascinated by an engraving of the Mad Hatter on the certificates. Mrs. Marshall told me she always allowed children to play with them when their parents were visiting her. That's why she had kept them through the years even though she realized they had lost any value they once had. I remember the lass having them spread out in the bedroom upstairs where she was playing. This was years ago, of course.''

A ringing of the phone brought McDonald to his feet.

"I know who that might be,'' Henry Spearman volunteered. "Morris Fain knows we are expected this morning, and I had left word that we might be staying here.''

"I'll get the phone. If it's Fain, I'll put you on.'' Jared Mcdonald left the sitting room and went into the hallway. Within five minutes he returned to his guests. He was animated.

"That was Sandor Gabor. He's a young tutor in economics at Clare. One of the bright prospects for our side, incidentally. He called to tell me he had just learned that G. Shepherd has been taken in for questioning by the police. Over Shepherd's vigorous protests, Gabor said. I don't know if you remember or not, but you two were with Shepherd at the Hales'. For all I know, you may have been in his shop. He's the best-known bookseller in town."

"Why would he be a suspect?" Henry Spearman interrogated.

"Maybe because he had opportunity, and a motive. For one thing, he was present at the Bentham dinner; in fact, Shepherd was with Hart just before he was found missing. For another, Hart had a valuable library. Shepherd was Hart's friend, or at least was thought to be. He ended up with almost all of Hart's books, at least everything of any value. And there were some very valuable rarities in the collection.

"Hart couldn't bear the thought of his books lying around in boxes gathering dust and losing much value in some warehouse while the bureaucratic wheels of probate turned. It was his wish that his books get into circulation quickly after his death and to that end he had made arrangements earlier with some influential lawyers that his entire estate be settled speedily.

"Shepherd had no sooner got his hands on his friend's books than there they were, packed into the front window of his shop. And at very fancy prices too. And there were posters in the front window announcing: PROVENANCE: HART. And when you went in, pointing up the stairs there were arrow signs saying: MORE HART. He might must as well have piped in some background music with the lyrics, 'You've gotta have Hart, miles and miles and miles of Hart.' It was all so opportunistic."

"Did they sell?" Henry Spearman asked.

"They've just gone on sale, but there's no doubt they're going to sell. Hart had them all: Smith, Ricardo, Mill, Marx. Mostly first editions. Some were presentation copies. He had some wonderful contemporary stuff, too. He had two first editions of Marshall. And a signed copy of *The General Theory*. How many of those do you see around?"

Henry Spearman was cleaning his glasses while listening to his friend's account. "So Shepherd benefited greatly from Hart's will by inheriting the books?"

"Not directly from his will. They were friends, but Shepherd was not the beneficiary. And he knew that there were no children or libraries that were going to get the books. Hart's collection would come up for sale at his death. And that's where Shepherd came in. As I said earlier, he got the whole collection, or all that was worth having.''

Henry Spearman put his glasses back on. ''Maybe I should visit the shop while I'm here. Is it off Market Square, Jared?''

''Yes, you could walk there from here. Just go to Market Square. You know where that is. And then ask anyone where Shepherd's is. They'll know. It's right near the Corn Exchange.''

''I recall Mr. Shepherd from the Hales' party,'' Pidge remarked. ''I don't think you met him, Henry. I didn't. But Ardis Horne pointed him out to us. He was the rather large man talking with the Indian economist you knew. The man who told me to simply call him Ajit.''

Henry Spearman did not respond. His curiosity satisfied, he had drifted into sleep.

Chapter 13:
The Cam Revisited

"Oh, you missed him, sir. He just went out. Not more than two minutes ago. Look, you can see him going under the bridge." The tall, angular, middle-aged man wearing a leather change purse on his belt pointed to a figure poling a punt that had just passed beneath the Silver Street Bridge. The Spearmans craned their necks over the edge of the dock and peered down the Cam at the retreating boat and its passenger-customers.

"He's not going to be back for an hour, if you ask me. Sometimes people don't like the trip, and they ask to come back early. But that's not often. Especially on a day like this. No, I'd say an hour." The dock manager of the punt rental business at the base of Mill Lane looked at the two Americans.

"But there's no need for you to wait," he added. "I've got other chauffeurs who are free now. Their boats are all the same, and the trip'll be the same. You can go straightaway if you like. I can't say that all the time. Sometimes we get queues going back to the University Centre."

"No, we'll wait," Henry Spearman responded. "We have heard about Mr. Pipes, and he's the one we want."

"It's up to you, guv'nor. You can take a seat on the bench by the river. I'll watch for Steve when he gets back."

"If you don't mind, we'll use the time to visit Peterhouse. We'll plan to return in an hour." Spearman was looking at his watch.

"That would make it about . . . ahh . . . 4 o'clock. Would that be satisfactory?"

"Maybe so, maybe not. If Steve comes back early, and there's a customer waiting, he's got to go out. We don't make anything just standing around."

"Your point's well taken," Henry Spearman replied. "I'll tell you what. Should Mr. Pipes come back before we return, you can start charging me from that point in time until we arrive back here. Start the meter as soon as he's back, whether we're here or not, is what I'm saying. I understand the value of opportunities foregone. I won't even expect you to discount the waiting charge by the cost of wear and tear the punt otherwise would receive."

The dock manager looked at Henry Spearman with his brow furrowed. He was uncertain if he was talking with a smart aleck or an egghead. After a pause for consideration, he said, "Fair enough. Except you need to pay me for the hour now, in advance. Then I'll know you're coming back."

"At least you know it's more likely," Henry commented, as he took some currency from his wallet. "Now, be sure Mr. Pipes waits. He's the one we want to have."

The Spearmans left the dock of one of Cambridge's several punt-rental establishments. Morris Fain had told them which location he had used. And he told them the name of the chauffeur who had impressed him so much: Steven Pipes.

It was still the day of their arrival in England. The Spearmans had napped at Jared McDonald's house and then got up for the purpose of this excursion. Pidge pulled from her suitcase a culotte and a middy blouse to wear and then put on a pair of espadrilles. She also found her nylon windbreaker to bring along against the chance it turned cool on the river. Henry put on the pair of oxfords he had worn on the plane from Boston, after extracting from his luggage a pair of Bermuda shorts and his favorite Lacoste shirt. From the table before they left, he picked up his camera and a small leather notebook.

"Do you think we'll pass for an English couple?" he quipped to Pidge as they left the house.

"Not even if we were on bicycles," was the response.

While waiting for Pipes's return, their interlude at Peterhouse was a pleasant one. They had not visited this Cambridge college during their previous visit. When the porter at Peterhouse learned the Spearmans were the guests of a Fellow at Bishop's College, he readily admitted them into the small interior quadrangle of the facility, even though regular visiting hours were over.

"Which is your own university, sir?" The porter asked Henry, from his booth just inside the Porter's Lodge.

"Harvard," Henry replied.

"Oh, he's a Cambridge man, Mr. Harvard was. From Emmanuel. One of our own fellows here, sir, a Mr. Kitch, was at Harvard. Told me the university's even in a town called Cambridge. I don't suppose you know him—Mr. Kitch, I mean?"

"No, I'm afraid I don't," Henry replied.

"We understand Peterhouse is the oldest college at Cambridge. Do you know when it began?" Pidge inquired.

"I'd be out of a job if I couldn't answer that one, ma'am. 1284. Almost seven centuries ago. Now tell me, when did your college begin?"

"1639, I believe," Pidge paused to think. "Yes, I think that's correct."

"Oh, Harvard's just a young pup then," the porter replied seriously.

The Spearmans thanked the porter for his courtesy and began their walk about the interior of the Peterhouse cloister. After examining the ancient chapel and circling the lawn and gardens, they made their way back to Mill Lane and down to the vicinity of the dock.

As they approached their destination, they heard the rental manager call out to them, "He's here. Steve Pipes is waiting for you."

Fain's description was accurate. Steve Pipes was a strapping young man. He was wearing black trousers, a white, long-sleeved shirt, and a gray vest with waist tabs. Pipes had a shock of light brown hair and a white complexion. The rainy summer had deterred his getting a tan, notwithstanding the outdoor nature of his work. Also, once on the water, Pipes placed a skimmer on his head, which afforded him additional protection from the sun.

"Of course I remember Mr. Fain," Pipes said with a broad smile as he was introduced to the Spearmans on the dock and learned of their connection with his former passenger. "There are some customers you never forget. The ones who tip a lot, for

example. But you especially remember the ones who almost die
in your punt! That incident didn't cause your friend to forswear
punting, did it?''

"No, I don't think so. He told me you were interested in economics. So, let's just say the law of diminishing marginal utility
applies robustly to Morris Fain when it comes to punting. Something like an appendectomy. Once you've derived utility from the
first one, there's not a lot to be gained from a second.''

"I see," Pipes said with a laugh. "Very good. Well, my boss
told me you're being charged since I got back with my last passengers. So, we should be going. Do you want to take on another
couple, before we push off?'' Steve asked. "It's a bit cheaper for
you if you do, and there's plenty of room. We are allowed to take
up to six in this boat.''

The Spearmans nixed the offer and so Pipes helped just the two
of them on board. He pushed the long, narrow boat away from
the dock with his hand and then stood erect in the back and
began poling.

"Anytime you want to try poling, you're welcome to," Pipes
said. "I'm not trying to shirk, mind you. It's just that some customers want to try.''

"You'll find neither of us will try to work you out of a job,"
Henry said. "What we want you to do is take us on the precise
route you took Morris Fain a couple weeks ago. I don't expect
another dumbbell from the sky, of course. But I would like you
to describe to us everything that happened to the two of you that
day. I gather from Morris it was just the two of you in the boat,
is that correct?''

"Oh yes, sir. I offered him the same option I did you—to share
with others. But he said he wanted to go alone. I remember we
were very busy that day, but he said he wanted to be the only
passenger. As far as I remember, he said he'd just arrived in
England and was tired. He looked tired, too. But most Americans
do, their first day here. So I didn't find that strange at all.''

Steve Pipes propelled the boat among the busy punt traffic on
this portion of the river. Soon they passed under the cars, coaches,
and bicycles that traveled above them on Silver Street. As his punt
came alongside Queens' College, he announced: "I'll be happy to
tell you about all the attractions on the way. But Mr. Fain asked

me just to give him the highlights. So if you want to replicate his ride, that's all I'll do. I remember he requested the 'Reader's Digest' version of what we passed."

The Spearmans agreed to take the same version.

Pidge settled back somewhat, taking a relaxed posture in the seat. Henry remained ramrod straight beside her on the punt's bench. Both looked to the stern, facing Pipes, from the bench closest to Pipes, because this was the way Steve had described Fain's location in the boat.

"You'll be sure to tell us when we approach where the accident occurred," Henry reminded their chauffeur.

"That's some way up, sir. Past the Backs and King's Chapel. Don't worry, you'll see everything. There's only one route and the punts go slow. You'll see everything—whether you want to or not. You can't pick and choose what you see when punting on the Cam. It's Hobson's choice."

Henry Spearman's ears pricked up. "Steve, in the States, one occasionally hears that expression. It means, as I understand it, no choice at all. That always intrigued me, as an economist. Didn't the phrase originate out of Cambridge? I think there's some connection."

Pipes smiled down at the Spearmans. "Yes, there's a connection. Funny, nobody's asked me about that in quite a while. Thomas Hobson was the man's name. In the 1600s he ran the stables in Cambridge and rented out horses and riding gear to the scholars. Made a lot of money at it, too, you might be interested to learn. Milton even mentions Hobson in a poem. 'Here lies old Hobson, Death has broke his girt'—I think I know a few more lines.

"Someone, I'm not sure anyone knows who, named 'Hobson's choice' after the man. It was Richard Steele, in the eighteenth century, who popularized the term outside Cambridge."

"But what was the reason behind the term?" Pidge asked. "I saw the plaque about his stables, but it wasn't clear to me."

"I can only tell you what Steele wrote. Hobson had a sizable livery operation, with lots of horses. But apparently whenever a scholar went there to rent a horse, Hobson always made him take the horse which stood next to the stable door, however much the person might have liked a different horse he'd ridden before.

Steele said you always got the horse that happened to be nearest the door. And so he said it was a proverb in Cambridge that when your selection was forced upon you by chance, the way Hobson did, you were to say, 'Hobson's choice.' ''

Henry Spearman was silent for a moment, his head bowed as if in a silent prayer. Then he looked up. ''Steele didn't understand the economics of what Hobson was trying to do. So often, Steve, in economics there's a hidden logic to what goes on. Steele missed the hidden logic behind Hobson's livery operation. I'm not surprised that Hobson was wealthy.''

''What do you mean, Dr. Spearman? Couldn't Hobson have made more money by giving his customers what they wanted?''

''That depends,'' Spearman replied. ''Depends on the costs to Hobson. Let's say Cambridge students treated horses they don't own the way lots of people treat rental cars they don't own: they drive them hard. Hobson has to watch out for that. What's one way to conserve his most valuable business assets? Always rent the horse that is the freshest, the horse that was ridden hard the longest ago.

''My prediction, Steve, is that if you were to do some research on Mr. Thomas Hobson, you would find that nothing was left to chance—for him or his customers. His horses were moved, stall by stall, down the barn, so the freshest horse always was closest to the door. This became the horse the next customer found to be 'Hobson's choice.' Oh, it was Hobson's choice, all right. But his choice had a logic to it.''

''Henry, I think that's enough. Remember we came to hear from our guide, not from you,'' Pidge half-kidded, half-admonished her husband.

As they spoke, the boat made its way along the river, gliding almost noiselessly past the sights and scenery that Fain and millions of other visitors to Cambridge over the years, have drunk in. Pipes began to entertain the Spearmans, but not with dates-and-places-type history. He had the knack of attaching stories about great Cambridge characters into his travelogue.

''Are you sure you want to be an economist?'' Pidge questioned their young chauffeur along the way. ''You have a real knack for history, it seems.''

''No, ma'am. I'm sure I don't want to be a historian. History is fun. But there are people with degrees in history chauffeuring punts for an occupation. Not that that's what they hoped to do. But it's the best they can do, so they claim. I want someday to do research in economics. There are no economists doing punt trips—at least, that I've ever seen.

"Are any of your students doing work like this, Professor Spearman?"

Henry Spearman came out of his reverie and replied, "Not that I know of. Of course, the opportunities are more limited in the States for exactly this type of work. It would take a very long pole to propel a punt on the Charles river along the campuses of Harvard and MIT. But even if it could be done, I suspect most of my students would be doing something more lucrative."

"That doesn't mean it's more enjoyable, Henry," Pidge objected.

"You're right, of course," he said, turning his head towards Pidge. "How much a person *makes* at a job, economists have a pretty good handle on measuring. How much a person *enjoys* a job is a tougher variable to quantify."

"Isn't one a proxy for the other?" Pipes volunteered. "I would enjoy my job more if my pay were doubled."

"The problem is, you'd also enjoy your job more if your workload were halved and your pay stayed the same."

Henry and Steve Pipes batted this topic back and forth for a few minutes. Pipes so relished the opportunity to talk economics with an economics professor who took an interest in him that he found it difficult to deliver his travelogue. Here he was, engaged in discussion with an economist whose work he had heard about. He knew Spearman could be helpful in advising him what he should be reading to prepare for graduate study.

But Pipes also understood the idea of enlightened self-empowerment. The Spearmans did not come here to counsel Steve Pipes. They had a different objective. He did not want to disappoint these particular passengers. It was best not to appeal to the Spearmans' benevolence but rather (a strategic thought) "address ourselves not to their humanity but their self love" as Adam Smith said.

"Your friend started to seem very relaxed about now," Pipes commented. "I still remember when we went under the bridge at Garret Hostel Lane—that's it, just ahead of us—he was lying somewhat back on the bench, taking in the scenery, and asking me occasional questions along the way. Mostly, though, I did the talking.''

Pipes paused. ''Incidentally, if you're interested, the rest of the guides and I consider where we are now as being just short of the halfway mark—at least for a fare we're taking up to Magdalene College and back. That's the ride your friend had paid for: to Magdalene and back. That's what most tourists want to do. That way they see the Backs, King's Chapel, and the Bridge of Sighs. Oh, and the Mathematical Bridge, too. That's what most people know about when they first get here. Those four attractions.''

A shadow fell across the boat as it passed beneath the bridge that connected the Backs with the colleges of Trinity and Trinity Hall. As the threesome emerged from under the bridge, Henry pulled out his small notebook, opened it, and said to Pipes:

''Now, Steve, I know it has been a while. But before you show us where the dumbbell fell and give us your account of what took place, I'd like you to listen to each of these questions carefully. If you want me to explain any of them, let me know. I'll be happy to do that.'' Henry Spearman then put the following interrogatories to his young admirer, giving Pipes an opportunity to respond to each one of them in turn:

''When you left the dock with Fain, was there anyone who seemed to be watching you, or anything unusual about your departure?''

''When you got back, I understand the police were involved and you talked to them. But did you notice anyone else around the dock looking suspicious?''

''As you went along the river, before or after the incident, did you notice anyone onshore following you along the bank?''

''As you went along the river, either before or after the incident, did you notice anyone in another punt following you or seeming to trace your path?''

''You said Morris Fain looked tired. Did he seem anxious or expecting danger in any way?''

''Did you see anyone on shore or in a boat who seemed to be pointing out your punt to someone, or pointing Morris Fain out?''

''When you went under the bridges prior to the incident—like the one we just passed—did you ever see anyone above, on any of them, who seemed to be watching or threatening you, or looking like they might be preparing to drop something on you?"

"Was there anything at all that day on the river that gave you any signal of what happened?"

The answer to each of Henry Spearman's questions was a 'No.' Pipes could not recall anything out of the ordinary that afternoon until the dumbbell almost killed Morris Fain.

"Now here's where you want to pay special attention," Pipes said, after responding to the last of Spearman's questions. "Right about now."

Pipes directed the Spearmans' attention straight ahead. Pidge and Henry turned in their seats toward the bow of the punt. "I remember Mr. Fain spotting the Bridge of Sighs. You see it in front of us. I'm not sure he knew what it was. But he seemed really interested. More interested than in anything we'd passed. But by now, as I said, he seemed relaxed and enjoying himself. I told him a couple stories about the bridge—its counterpart in Venice, and all that. But I remember he was interested in the bars over the windows on the bridge. Not that that's unheard of. Every now and then, someone asks about them. It's not a hard question to answer. They were used to keep St. John's undergraduates from sneaking in after gate hours. But your friend, he wanted to know about those bars. I remember that."

"And then what happened—as you recall?" Henry asked.

"Well, when I saw he was interested in the bridge, I tried to steer directly for the center of the arch. I do that partly so my customers can get a good angle if they're taking photographs and they want the bridge in the middle of the shot. You know, I can't remember whether Mr. Fain had a camera or not. But that's the reason I usually draw the punt up alongside St. John's. I'm going to do that for you, too, in a minute. You'll see what I mean."

"Now, am I to understand that even though Morris Fain did not have a camera, you still took him close alongside the building up ahead? Why is that?"

Pipes tried not to act defensive. "Well, as I say, I'm not sure now whether your friend had a camera. He may have; maybe he didn't. All I meant was if I notice they don't have a camera, I'm probably less likely to pull as close in to the wall as we're going to go. It can depend on other things. If there's another punt there, I'll take a different angle. Sometimes the river is so busy, I'll be on the opposite side, just to get through. It just happened that that day we came right alongside. I remember, I could touch the wall.''

"And I gather you saw nothing about to happen?"

"Oh, no sir. If I did, I wouldn't have gone where I went. I can get into trouble if a punt gets damaged. If my boss thinks it is my fault, it comes straight from my pay.''

Pipes nudged the boat up a little bit more, toward the river wall of St. John's college. There were no other boats in the place where the punt seemed headed. Pipes became silent. Henry asked no more questions. Everyone in the punt was all eyes, and the eyes were all looking up.

"Well, here we are. Doesn't look as if there'll be any excitement this time.'' Pipes stopped the punt and placed his hand on the wall of the College to hold the punt motionless.

"I'll move away if you're superstitious. Otherwise I'll stay. I don't mind either way. I've been this way a hundred times since the accident with nothing happening. I think it was one of those once-in-a-million kind of things. That's what I believe now. But when it happened, I wasn't as ready to write it off like that.''

"This is where the dumbbell fell,'' Pipes continued. "As near as I can tell, if it dropped straight down, it must have had to come from one of these two windows.'' Pipes was pointing to a second- and third-floor window.

"If someone actually threw it at Mr. Fain, it could have come from a couple of other windows to the side. I'd have thought I'd have spotted someone hanging out to throw the dumbbell from the side. And then there's the roof. It might have come from the roof. Nobody knows that either. But let me stress that I had no reason to be looking up. When you're guiding a punt, you're usually looking at the water, not the sky. I usually only look up when someone asks me to identify some bird. But since the incident, I confess I tend to look up everytime I pass St. John's.''

"Check me on this if I am mistaken, Steve,'' Henry asked. Spearman was now standing in the punt, staring hard at the brick wall and fenestration above him. "You told Morris Fain you might have seen something come from a third-floor window, am I correct?''

"Yes."

"That something you thought you saw—was it a person?"

"I can't say. I really can't. It may have been my imagination. The dumbbell came down in a blur. When I looked up a minute later, after getting my punt away from the wall, I saw that two of the windows directly above us were open. In my mind, I may have put the two together and imagined what wasn't there."

"Were the open windows a surprise to you?"

"The windows being open don't tell me anything. It's summer. As you can see, they're open today."

Henry Spearman sat back down in the punt, beside Pidge and facing Steve Pipes.

"Well, what do you think, sir?" Pipes asked.

"It was either an accident, or it was deliberate," Spearman replied softly, looking up at the young man. "Those are the only two hypotheses. It makes a world of difference which one we select. Obviously, I hope it was an accident. Unfortunately, I have no control over which hypothesis is true. You see, Steve, in finding the truth, I'll have no alternative. Ultimately, it's Hobson's choice."

Pidge looked up at Steve Pipes and shrugged her shoulders: "What does *that* mean?"

Chapter 14:
The Poor Yank

"Had a bit of a celebrity yesterday in my punt, Mum—at least, to me he's famous." Steve Pipes was spreading marmalade on some breakfast toast his landlady had placed before him. Dappled sunlight shone through lace curtains into the breakfast nook where Mrs. Saltmarsh was pouring her second cup of coffee that morning.

"A film star?" Mrs. Saltmarsh guessed.

Pipes chuckled out loud. "I don't think you'd confuse him with Alec Guinness. But in economics he's a star."

Mrs. Saltmarsh returned to the table, steaming cup of coffee in hand, and sat down. "Oh, a big brain, is he?"

"You might put it that way. A professor at Harvard in America—his name is Spearman. I had him and his wife as customers yesterday morning. They had never been in a punt before. They are friends of the chap who rode in my punt and almost got hit by the dumbbell a couple of weeks ago. They wanted me to take them to the exact place on the river where the accident was. Then, on our way back, they wanted to stop there again. I kept looking up when we were there, I can tell you! You know, now I look up every time I go past St. John's."

"Well, you should, dearie," Mrs. Saltmarsh interjected. "That other dumbbell might come crashin' down. You never know, these days. I told you about my neighbor in Clapham who dropped the vase out her window? I always thought she could do the same thing again. Maybe not a vase next time. But something."

"Well, what made them interesting passengers for me was talking about economics with the professor. I told him I had wanted to come here to study, but didn't get in; that I read everything I could and hoped someday to go to a Redbrick university after I'd worked awhile. He seemed impressed with what I knew—we talked a lot about Joan Robinson's work and a book I had read by McDonald, who it turns out is a good friend of Spearman's—and he told me he'd help me get on to a graduate course in America. If I ever wanted to, that is. He and his wife also lapped up everything I told them about academic life here. They seemed surprised at what I knew. But I told them that you could learn a lot as a punt chauffeur—if you kept your ears open."

"Will this man give a lecture while he's here?" Mrs. Saltmarsh inquired.

"No, he gave a lecture when he was here before."

"Well, I'm glad you had some nice customers yesterday, luv. I know you get down a bit when people are rude. So many people are nowadays."

"Oh, there was nothing rude about these Americans. They spent quite a bit of the afternoon with me. She was keen on Cambridge history. And he was much more friendly to me than a Cambridge don. I've heard that about American profs. There's not such a gap between them and the students. The best thing is, I'll see them again."

"How's that, luv?"

"At the dock, I told them that they should see some of the country around Cambridge and I suggested they come to Grantchester, and I'd show them around the village for free. His wife wants to see the river in the country, so I told her, 'there's nowhere better than where I live.' They're taking a motorcar out here later this afternoon."

"Oh, Steve, I wish you'd let me know earlier. I'm not sure I'm up to talking to some pie-in-the-sky professor." Mrs. Saltmarsh's face took on a look of concern.

"Mum, don't worry about a thing. If you meet them, you'll really like them both. He won't just talk economic theory with you. They both seem interested in Cambridge, and they'd like to see our area."

With a twinkle in his eye, Steve added, "Tell you what, you can tell him your theory about Professor Hart's death. Professor

Spearman's interested in that. He was full of questions about the Hart murder.''

"Well, I should think so.''

"Strangely enough, they had just visited the University of London shortly before the murder, and they went there especially to see Bentham in his case.''

"Better things to do in London than that, I'd tell 'em. Imagine, all the way from America to see a corpse in a box!''

"Actually, they only stopped off in London briefly. Their main business was in Cambridge. In fact, he was not here primarily to give a lecture. He was here to buy a house.''

"Buy a house?'' Mrs. Saltmarsh asked.

"Well, not in the conventional sense. He and his wife are not planning to move from America. He hopes to buy the house that was once owned by another—as you put it—'big brain', one of the biggest brains Cambridge ever had, at least in economics. Do you know the big house on Madingley Road near Magdalene?''

Mrs. Saltmarsh nodded, more out of politeness to her boarder than out of assurance on her own part.

"That was Alfred Marshall's. Spearman hopes to buy that home—not for himself, as I understand it, but for some wealthy Yanks who want to preserve it. The idea is to choose a young American economist and put him there for a year, pay him a stipend and all his expenses, give him no duties, and hope he'll be inspired by his surroundings.''

Mrs. Saltmarsh thought she had heard everything. "Is the house empty now?''

"Oh no. Mr. Thring, a Fellow at St. John's, lives there now. He bought it from Mrs. Marshall's estate about twenty years ago.''

"Lived there twenty years, has he?''

"That's what Professor Spearman told me.''

"And what's he done so inspirin'?'' her tone of sarcasm took her young lodger aback.

"I don't know,'' Steve admitted.

"Well, he's had twenty years to come up with something. And the poor Yank only gets a year? Better not expect too much out of him.''

Chapter 15:
Balliol Croft Regained

Henry Spearman knew it had to be his imagination. But somehow, in his mind's eye, when he first visited Balliol Croft with Pidge and Morris Fain—when they had first hesitantly walked up the drive together—the place seemed to have a congenial air about it, the way a nursery can look expectant months before the baby actually arrives. To Spearman, on that morning two weeks ago, Balliol Croft had looked like it was anticipating a new life. Henry thought at the time that Pidge and Morris shared this same sense of happy expectation.

Today, Balliol Croft seemed to have a gloom about it. It was not that of a haunted house—Hollywood style. To Spearman, there was nothing eerie about the place. But there seemed to be an angst hovering about the house and grounds. Probably, Spearman thought to himself, this was simply the anxiousness he felt in his own heart about the events that had followed their initial attempt to purchase the property.

It was one thing not to be able to buy something because someone else bid more for it. "In markets, resources go to their most highly valued use." *That*, Spearman understood. How many times had those very words spilled from his lips in a Harvard classroom? Hundreds of times over, he knew. Today, there was a kind of emptiness to the concept of efficient allocation.

It appeared now that Fain's foundation might in fact get Balliol

Croft. The main rival for the home had dropped out of the bidding. But Spearman knew it was hardly a voluntary dropping out, of the kind he was accustomed to teaching in the theory of price. In economic analysis, when someone quit bidding, it was because the price was too high—relative to the bidder's income. It was not because the bidder was killed before the market cleared.

"Morning, Henry. I hope you slept well. Did you have a good flight over?" Morris Fain had come up silently behind Spearman as the economist stood in the driveway near the front of Balliol Croft.

"I slept very well, thanks. Pidge and I took a nap yesterday after we arrived. That helped. We are physically refreshed. But I must say, we are both a little uneasy about this trip. I'm not looking forward to negotiating with Duncan Thring again. I feel sorry for the man. It's not just that he has come back to us after the Hart deal ended. But, as I recall, he was an acquaintance of Hart's."

"I'm not finding this enjoyable myself," Fain said. "Something happened to me yesterday that was very unpleasant. I want to talk to you about it. But it can wait until after we see Thring. I think he's expecting us, so we should go on in."

Duncan Thring greeted the two Americans at the side door. If there was anything troubling his soul that morning, Spearman could not detect it through the man's stolid British affability.

"Do c-c-come in, gentlemen," Thring said. He held open the screen door and beckoned the two Americans into his home. "I'm grateful to you for coming here. We could have m-m-met in my rooms at College. But Mr. Fain, you said you'd like to see the house again. And we can be more c-c-comfortable talking here."

Duncan Thring led his two guests into Balliol Croft's living room. Coffee already had been prepared and was awaiting them on the glass-topped table. A basket of pastries wrapped in cloth accompanied the hot beverage.

"Do make yourself comfortable. Sit anywhere you like," Thring said, as he selected the wooden rocking chair.

"Now then, how should we proceed?"

Morris Fain took over the conversation at this point. "We know you originally rejected our offer for the purchase of Balliol Croft. I won't pretend, sir, that we weren't disappointed. But we knew when we first had the idea of returning this home to a Marshallian heritage that we might not be successful. And we knew the impact of Marshall's writings didn't depend upon his home becoming an economics study center of some sort. Still, I guess we all had our hopes up.

"And then I got your letter. Let me say, Professor Thring, I appreciated the gentle way you let us down. But we were disappointed nonetheless. You know how it is, I'm sure. Once you get your sights set on something, you're never the same if you don't attain it."

Fain paused briefly to join Spearman and Thring in enjoying some of the morning repast their host had set out. "I realize, of course, that you had cut a deal with Dr. Hart to buy your house. And we all know that your reasons were only partly financial: you wanted to keep Balliol Croft within the Cambridge academic community.

"I also know Dr. Hart was a friend of yours. I've not had an opportunity personally to express my sympathy over that sad event." Henry Spearman nodded his head in Thring's direction, as if to affirm what his colleague was saying. "But the death of Dr. Hart, sad as that is, doesn't change our desire to have Balliol Croft, though it does make it more awkward.

"We know the reputation Americans often have in Europe. Whether they deserve it or not, I can't say. But we don't want to appear to be taking advantage of your situation. It's just that, for us, our objective remains unchanged.

"We do not want to take advantage of the loss of your buyer. I flew Professor Spearman back again because I thought he could best handle any concerns you may still have about our intention to use this home in a way we think you'd find satisfactory.

"We realize, or course, you may decide to put the house on the market again. Perhaps you have another Cambridge party in mind for the home. Perhaps you now plan to stay here. But we're prepared to offer the same price we did before, providing we can have occupancy in short order."

"Well, I'll tell you, gentlemen. This m-m-may surprise you. But I hope pleasantly. I am ready to s-s-sell. Indeed, I am eager to do so, and move on. Nigel's death affected me deeply. I know his being murdered had nothing to do with his plan to move. I

take c-c-c-consolation from that. But when you g-g-g-get to be
my age, you lose some resilience. Your stamina declines. I suppose
you're both too young to know what I'm talking about." Thring
paused and took a sip of coffee from his cup.

"And there's another matter that now affects this decision. My
children would tell me I'm foolish to tell you this. But I think
you should know. Someone broke into my house last night. About
eleven. That has upset me. I've lived here all these years and
nothing like that has ever happened before." Thring pushed his
fingers through his thick gray hair. "The house just isn't the same
to me any more."

Both Spearman and Fain had been listening to their host, but
this news intensified their concentration.

"Did the police catch the burglar?" Spearman asked.

"No, *I* almost did. N-n-n-not that I could have detained the
culprit, mind you. What happened is that I f-f-found an intruder
in the house. Tuesday nights, you see, I always go to High Table
at St. John's. Every Tuesday. Done so for years. Even when my
wife was alive. After dinner, some of the Fellows—always the
same group—meet in the Senior Common Room to talk. You
know how it is. We g-g-get to talking, and before you know it,
it's l-l-late evening.

"So I left St. John's to come home after our port and conversation. I was walking, of course. I never bicycle at night. Too
dangerous.

"I came up my driveway and noticed a light on in the attic.
Now I always leave a light on in the sitting room when I leave—
but the attic? When I got to the front duh-duh-door, I n-n-noticed
it was ajar. I don't ever lock up—the children tell me I should,
and I know they're right, of course. But I hate to see the world
come to that. At one time we didn't even lock our college rooms.

"Now, where was I? Oh, yes. I went in, and I called out, 'who's
there?' And the next thing I knew I heard someone running down
the stairs, through the hall, and out through the side door. I got a
glimpse of someone, but just the back. Whoever it was almost ran
through the door. You know—the door we just came in." Thring
gestured to the side door with the hand which was holding his
coffee cup. "By the time I went out to the front, whoever it was
was gone. Probably through the bushes at the side of the house."

"Was anything missing, that you know of, or any damage done to the house?" Fain asked, leaning forward in his chair as if to study the front of Thring's face. Spearman also was watching Thring closely.

"N-nothing was m-missing. At least, as far as I know. Whoever it was was moving so f-f-fast that I don't see how that person could have been carrying anything. Not at th-th-that speed. I never found any damage. The p-police came round—they were here in an instant after I rang—and they p-poked all around the house and never found anything amiss.

"They looked outside, too—I'm sure they disturbed the neighbors, what with their f-f-f-flashlights and everything. B-b-but I couldn't help that. I talked to them all this m-m-morning, of course, and told them what happened."

Morris Fain was the next to speak. "I had planned to tell Henry about this later, after we left. But I'll mention it now. My hotel room was broken into yesterday evening."

At this, Henry's eyes widened as he turned in the direction of Fain. Thring looked more sad than surprised at this news.

"Morris, you should have called me last night!" Spearman admonished. "You know I've been concerned about your safety since Hart's death."

"I didn't call you, Henry, because I didn't know how tired you'd be. Had you been staying at the hotel with me, I probably would have phoned you or stopped by. Also, I knew you were with a friend."

"Are you okay?"

"Oh, yes, I'm fine. In my case, I came back to my room from dinner. I had just eaten downstairs at the hotel. It was about nine-thirty. My door was locked. But someone had been in my room."

"How do you know th-th-that?" Thring asked.

"Did you have valuables in the room?" Spearman added before Fain could respond.

"Nothing was missing," Fain replied. "But something was added."

"Th-th-th-that's a change, for a thief," Thring stammered. "Usually it's the other w-w-way round."

"What did you find?" Spearman wanted to know.

"A note," Fain replied, reaching in his shirt pocket. He extracted a sheet of white paper which he had folded up. Fain straightened it and passed it first to Henry.

Spearman noted that it was English size cut paper, a tad longer than the standard 8 ½" by 11" paper used in the States. Henry knew about the size before this visit. His secretary had complained to him how difficult it was to file papers from England, because they either stuck out from an American manila folder or would not fit easily into an accordion file folder.

Spearman's eyes scanned four lines of text, handwritten, in block letters:

THE DUMBBELL IN SPRING
IS MEANT TO BRING
AN END TO FAIN
AND A SEASON OF RAIN

Henry then passed the note to Thring.

"This must be a j-joke, don't you think?" Thring said, after studying the sheet of paper. "Surely, no one who writes such doggerel can be serious." Thring gave the paper back to Fain, who placed it back in his pocket.

"I found it in my bathroom, right beside the sink," Fain explained. "I didn't notice anything else missing. I had my wallet and passport with me in the restaurant. I never travel with much cash. And I was wearing my watch, of course. So there wasn't much of value in the room.

"But a thief, even a disappointed one, wouldn't leave a note like this." Fain looked puzzled.

Henry Spearman looked concerned. "Morris, I don't think you can treat this as a joke," he said. "Before, I thought there probably was no connection between your wanting Balliol Croft, Hart's death, and your near miss with the dumbbell. Now, learning of the break-in here and the break-in at your hotel room, we can't be sure. You'll recall Pidge conjectured there could be a connection between an attempt on your life and the purpose of your being here. Professor Thring, you may recall that. It was here in your home." Thring nodded that he remembered.

Henry pointed to the note in Fain's shirt. "Have you showed that to the police?"

"No. If something had been missing from my room, I would have called the police. But for that note? What could they do? They haven't found Hart's murderer. Do you think they'll find who put a sheet of paper in my room?

"I did inquire at the desk if they could tell me who had a key to my room. They said 'just the service staff.' But that doesn't tell me a whole lot. If you look at the locks on hotel rooms in England, you'll see they aren't designed to be much more than an annoyance. You may remember, Henry, at the Blue Boar we were actually issued skeleton keys! The Arbor House, where I'm at now, is a bit better. But somebody didn't have any trouble getting in."

"I wonder if you shouldn't check out," Thring suggested. "Go to another hotel. Maybe the University Arms over on Re-re-gent Street. You won't have the r-river of course, but you've got P-p-Parker's Piece right nearby. I'd be surprised if the Arms didn't keep a customer's room secure.

"I tell you what. I'll ring them, if you like. Dealt with them for years." Thring started to rise from his rocking chair.

"No, just stay put," Fain objected. "I'm not going to change hotels. I'll just watch my backside—if you know the expression, Professor Thring." Their host sat back and began rocking, his hands positioned stiffly on the arms of the chair.

At this point, Henry Spearman spoke up. "The suggestion may not be a bad one—changing hotels, that is. If someone is trying to get at you, moving to a different location might put them off balance. I don't know what to make of the note, Morris. But if I were you, I would not treat it casually. I haven't been treating the punt incident casually."

"Well, as we say in the States, I'll take all this under advisement. Which usually seems to mean, 'I'll ignore what you say.' " Fain smiled at his two companions. "I said I wanted to look at parts of the house again. Do you mind, Professor Thring, if I do that?"

"No, of course not. Help yourself. I'll just clear up these cups and join you in a bit."

"I'll help you with those," Henry volunteered, as he began to assemble the cups and saucers. Thring thanked him, and the two academicians headed toward the kitchen—while Morris Fain headed toward the stairs.

In the kitchen, Spearman took Thring aside and spoke to him softly. "I appreciate the concern you showed about Morris Fain. As you can tell, my wife and I are concerned about him, too. We actually went to the Cam yesterday afternoon and traced his precise route on the river from the dock all the way to where the dumbbell fell, and back. We even hired the same chauffeur."

"You don't say!" Thring exclaimed. "And tell me, di-di-di-did anybody try to drop anything on your head?"

"No, there was no dumbbell. Nothing."

"Well, what a relief," Thring responded. "That's the way it sh-sh-should be, you know. F-f-fun. Punting is supposed to be fun, not d-d-dangerous."

"So you think it was an accident?" Spearman asked.

"Yes, and let me tell you why. It's the p-p-porters."

"The porters?" Spearman asked, wondering what they had to do with his question.

"Yes, let me tell my theory. The porters at St. John's never learned who dropped the d-d-dumbbell on your Mr. F-Fain. Now there's something about Cambridge porters that may surprise you: they eventually learn *everything* that's going on in a college. Even among the Fellows." Thring looked a bit sheepish in conceding this. "Th-th-the fact that the porters never c-c-caught the culprit makes me think it was an accident. If it was duh-done on purpose, then the ch-ch-chap's a clever one, he is."

The two men stacked the dishes in the kitchen and made their way upstairs. They found Fain in the attic and asked him how the inspection was going. Fain said he was about to make his way down to reconnoiter the upstairs rooms. He then made similar rounds on the main floor and finally made his way to the basement. "It looks like no tornadoes have been through since we were here last, Henry," he announced at the conclusion of his tour. "I doubt if anything's changed outside either. Professor Thring, I'm prepared to offer you a thousand pounds earnest money today, with the papers to be drawn up and signed in, shall we say, two days. The balance to be paid then. Do we have a deal?"

"Yes, I th-th-think we do."

As he handed over a check, Fain asked Thring gently when he would be able to leave.

"It may take a few weeks, but in the meantime you may have access to the house for your planning purposes. As long as you don't move things in until I'm moved out—that's all I ask."

"We could not ask for more," Fain said.

Henry and Morris made their way down the stone driveway to Madingley Road. Both felt a sense of relief, not only that they had at last made the acquisition, but that the negotiations had gone so affably.

Chapter 16:
Ya Got to Have Hart

Books. Henry Spearman never tired of them. If he had occasion to spend a few days in a college town or a large city, he made it a point to look over the offerings of secondhand dealers, browsing from store to store. Although Spearman was at G. Shepherd's on a serious matter, the additional utility he derived from finding in one place such a magnificent collection of great rarities in economics made the visit a pleasure, not a chore.

Through the glass of G. Shepherd's front window, the diminutive economist observed the books whose titles were visible to any passersby who happened to look in as they made their way along St. Edward's Passage, where Shepherd's store was located. This short alleyway, across the street from King's College, intersected with a tiny lane that led to the Arts Theatre and the Corn Exchange.

Shepherd's was a good location for a small specialty shop that could not afford the rent paid by the larger retailers on the busy streets that fronted the University's prominent sites. In his time, John Maynard Keynes also had found the location congenial. Although he had rooms at King's, he rented a flat above Shepherd's for his private comings and goings.

Jared McDonald's description of the display in Shepherd's window was accurate. Some pastel-colored cardboard signs, on which **PROVENANCE: HART** and **MORE HART INSIDE** were printed, intermingled with a scattering of rare volumes giving the impression that here was only a taste of what was available inside. And what an abundance of first editions there was to feast on! Both volumes of Wicksteed's *Common Sense of Political Economy*; Senior's *An Outline of the Science of Political Economy*; Edgeworth's *Mathematical Psychics*; Bowley's *Mathematical Groundwork of Economics*; James Mill's *Commerce Defended*.

As Spearman shoved open the door to the bookshop, his entrance was announced by the tinkling of a bell. He found himself in a small room where much of the interior space was taken up by shiny, waxed wooden tables with sunken shelves. They were packed with books whose spines faced upward from under glass top covers. These were the more valuable volumes.

Oak bookcases lined the walls from ceiling to floor, sectioned off by cardboard signs reading BIOGRAPHY; HISTORY; TRAVEL; THEATRE. Browsers were afforded easier access to these, the more pedestrian volumes.

A narrow, book-lined stairway with a marker in the shape of an arrow, pointing upward, led customers to the floor above. Printed on the sign were the words MORE HART.

The most striking feature of G. Shepherd's, Spearman thought, was its lack of clutter compared with other secondhand bookstalls he had known. Here there was no musty odor; the air seemed fresh; the books in the window and on the shelves were free of dust. Even where there wasn't enough shelf space for all of the books in one category, the overflow was placed in orderly stacks on the floor.

Gregory Shepherd sat on a high stool behind a glass top counter at the front of the shop. An unlit briar pipe was clenched between his teeth as he perused a catalogue. He was a heavy-set man, potbellied, with jowly cheeks of a bluish color that even a close shave could not remove. His head of thick gray hair was brushed straight back. Over a light green pullover he wore a tweed sports jacket with patched elbows. Henry Spearman recognized him from the Hales' party.

The shop's proprietor seemed unaware of Spearman's presence. The economist turned and began to examine some volumes with tooled leather bindings that stood upright on the oak shelves.

"Those are not meant for reading. Unless you're desperate. But they will improve the décor of almost any room.'' Gregory Shepherd had stepped noiselessly from behind the counter and come up beside the short browser in his shop.

Spearman turned to face him and was greeted with an outstretched arm. Henry returned the welcome. He shook the bookman's hand, and with a slight, apologetic smile, he explained, ''You seemed so preoccupied with the catalogue you were looking at, I decided not to disturb you.''

''Disturb me? Oh no! Don't put it that way. Customers are never a disturbance. One of my greatest pleasures is showing off my merchandise. Especially these days.'' Then he added, with a feigned air of conspiracy, ''This is the finest inventory I've had in thirty years in the business. Of course, I'm not talking about these morocco-bound things you've been looking at. They're strictly for show.''

''Yes, the Hart collection. I heard you acquired it. One of the best holdings of economic rarities in the world.''

They were interrupted by an anemic looking man with a scholarly stoop. He was tall and thin. Between his dark eyes was a thin, aquiline nose set above a hairline mustache. His hand was clutching a thick volume, which he had brought from upstairs and now wagged in front of Shepherd's face.

''How much are you asking for this?'' he inquired.

Shepherd took the book and opened it to its title page. After a glance, he replied, ''First edition of Marshall's *Principles* in fine condition. Quite hard to find—a real jewel. One hundred pounds.'' Shepherd handed the volume back.

''I've been looking for one of these for years. I've got all of Marshall's editions in their first printing except this one.'' He paused for a moment while he slowly riffled the pages of the book. Then he screwed up his eyes and peered at Shepherd. ''Is that price the best you can do for me?''

''I'm afraid so. If you want it, I suggest you take it. You're not likely to come across another soon. In this condition, they're scarce as hens' teeth.''

''I'll give you ninety-five pounds,'' the man countered.

''I appreciate your offer,'' Shepherd responded, ''but that's my last word. If you want to call back in a couple of weeks, perhaps

you could bring me down a bit. But I doubt if the book'll be
here then."

Spearman made a mental note about the customer's hapless bargaining skills. The man had let Shepherd know, at the outset, that
he had been looking for years to buy the item in G. Shepherd's
inventory. And if that were not enough, he told Shepherd that this
particular book would round out a collection he was trying to
complete. The man would be an easy mark in a Mideastern bazaar,
Spearman thought.

"All right, I'll take the book. But the price seems rather steep
to me. Will you take a check on a local bank? Barclay's?"

Shepherd nodded an okay and, after excusing himself from
Henry Spearman, led the Marshall purchaser to the front of the
store.

Meanwhile, as Spearman continued to browse, he noticed an
entrance to a room, much of it hidden by a partially closed curtain.
The economist, curious as usual, attempted to discover what was
inside. Through the crack he could see several small piles of books
neatly arranged on a badly faded rug. Seated at a small wooden
desk, in the far corner, was a plump and round-cheeked woman
with thick-lensed glasses and mouse-colored hair. She exuded an
air of lethargy and inefficiency as, through squinting eyes, she
slowly and laboriously played hunt-and-peck on her typewriter.

Spearman quietly squeezed through the curtain to get a better
view. He was interested in those books stacked so neatly on the
threadbare Oriental carpet. Were they part of the Hart acquisition?
If so, why weren't they on display in the outer rooms? It occurred
to Spearman that perhaps they were duplicates of books which
could command a higher price if they appeared rarer than they
really were. When Shepherd sold one copy, after a respectable
interval had passed he could replace it with another from his hidden stock. Such a strategy would bring him higher returns than
placing the full inventory in view. Spearman hoped to find evidence that would enable him to accept or reject his hypothesis.

The short economist wasn't sure if the room he had entered
surreptitiously was off limits. Perhaps it was meant to be closed
to all but the owner and his designated employees. On the other
hand, there was no sign warning customers to keep out. Spearman

began to tiptoe quietly between the book piles while he strained to get a glimpse of at least one title.

"Who gave you permission to come in here?" The typist had discovered the intruder. "You must leave immediately!" Her tone was severe.

"Terribly sorry," Spearman replied, showing his most disarming smile. "I wasn't aware that potential purchasers were excluded from seeing part of the merchandise."

"These items are not part of the merchandise, at least not the part that's for sale. Now you must leave or I shall call Mr. Shepherd." She seemed vehement. Henry decided to beat a hasty retreat.

As Spearman pushed his way back through the beige curtain, he saw that Gregory Shepherd was coming down the narrow stairway, followed closely by a man of about thirty-five who had broad shoulders and a bronzed face. The two men were in animated discussion. When the proprietor saw Spearman, he looked surprised.

"Dr. Spearman, I thought you had left. Allow me to introduce you to Herbert Grundy. He drove up from London to see the Hart collection."

"I'm honored to meet you, Dr. Spearman. I'm familiar with your work. So are my students. I'm a lecturer at the London School of Economics and I've seen to it your name is on their reading list."

"I wonder what your students did to deserve such punishment," Spearman said, his brow wrinkled, but his eyes twinkling.

"Some of them find your work tough going. But most of them find the material eye-opening—like a new way of thinking. Maybe the Marxists in the class would agree it's punishment. I've never asked." Grundy had an easy way of talking, although his high-pitched voice seemed incongruent with his rugged appearance.

Spearman smiled at the admiring young economist and expressed his thanks. Then a thought occurred to him and he abruptly changed the subject. "Which of Hart's books do you find most enticing?"

Grundy, at first taken aback, nevertheless responded quickly. "I was hoping to find a first edition of Marshall, but I understand I missed it by only a few minutes. Still, I wouldn't at all mind owning a first edition of William Stanley Jevons's *Theory of Political Economy*. There's an absolute gem upstairs, but it's a presentation copy to his sister, and it's priced beyond my reach.''

Spearman turned toward Shepherd. "I'm curious, Mr. Shepherd, do you have mixed feelings when someone, like Mr. Grundy here, decides *not* to purchase an item like that? Or to turn the question around, do you feel some pangs of regret when you part with an edition of a great classic, perhaps especially one inscribed by the author himself?"

The book dealer replied unhesitatingly.

"That's an easy question to answer. An interesting one, too. My deepest feeling is one of relief when a valuable book goes out through the door. At least if it's been purchased at or very near my asking price. If it's an inscribed copy, you can rest assured it cost me a pretty penny at the auction. With all the expert collectors and dealers in attendance, the bidding sometimes gets frantic for the really choice items. One can get carried away by the excitement and end up having to take losses on the most valuable acquisitions.

"When Nigel's library came up for sale in London, the auction attracted dealers from all over the world. And when the presentation copy of Keynes's *General Theory*, inscribed to Hart himself, came on the market, the atmosphere in the room was so highly charged that an elderly collector I know from the Cotswolds began to hyperventilate.

"As it happens, I had to outbid the head of one of the largest banks in Germany for that morsel. It was nice to get it, but the competition was fierce. The amount I paid would enable me to stock my everyday inventory for three months. No, Dr. Spearman, I'd be delighted if Mr. Grundy wanted to take that burden off my hands."

"A burden to you may be a bargain to me," Herbert Grundy said. He had been listening with some restlessness. "I'll just look around a bit more upstairs and see if I can come up with something attractive—and affordable—before I set out for London. I'm still a bit miffed about losing out on that Marshall volume. Bit of bad luck, that." He excused himself and headed in the direction of the narrow stairway.

When Grundy was out of earshot, Shepherd bent his head toward Spearman's and, in a voice barely above a whisper, said,

"Dr. Spearman, I wonder if I might have a word with you in private. I need your advice on a delicate matter."

"Sure," Spearman responded sympathetically. "How may I be of help?"

Shepherd grasped Spearman's arm and accompanied him to a far corner of the room where no browsers were in evidence. In a low voice he continued the conversation. "Perhaps you've heard that the police consider me a suspect in the murder of Nigel Hart. Quite ridiculous, of course, but it doesn't seem funny to me. I was even taken in for questioning, and was allowed to go home only because my solicitor's indignant protests scared them off."

"Did they tell you *why* you are a suspect?" Spearman inquired.

"They didn't tell me much. Just asked a great many questions and made cryptic comments, innuendos—that sort of thing. But I got the impression they believe I had a powerful motive for dispatching Nigel."

"Which was . . . ?"

"To acquire his books," Shepherd explained. "And then, you see, it's all compounded by the fact that I attended the Bentham Society's do the night of Nigel's death. It's so upsetting. And to think I almost cried off from the dinner this year because I had been feeling a bit queasy the day before. It was Nigel who said I just *must* be there; that it wouldn't be the same without me. And besides, he had some new books in his collection that he wanted to show me and just *couldn't* wait for my reaction."

The economist looked at the book dealer. Shepherd's face had taken on a worried expression.

Spearman was puzzled.

"You said you wanted my advice, but it's not clear what kind of counsel you want. I'm an economist, not an attorney."

"I know that. But attorneys I already have. Perhaps I'm just grasping at straws, but I feel I need the advice of someone who is not only intelligent and learned, but also, by reputation, wise. Wisdom, as you economists might say, is an increasingly scarce resource. I know you have some ties in Cambridge. And you are involved, indirectly, with Nigel Hart, because both of you were once pursuing the same house. From your experience here, as an outsider but not quite, do you have any wisdom for me?"

"Adam Smith, a *truly* wise economist, said that if you want to understand another human being, you must put yourself in that person's shoes. That's the only way we can sympathize with someone else. So I ask myself, how would I react if I were in your situation?"

"And the answer?" Shepherd asked expectantly.

"By doing nothing."

"What do you mean?"

"I can assure you, Mr. Shepherd, that the police have nothing on you. The fact that you were in close proximity to Nigel Hart on the night of his murder in no way implicates you in the crime. Every other guest had the same opportunity."

"But I had a motive!" Shepherd said in exasperation.

"His books?" Spearman offered.

Shepherd nodded gravely.

Spearman made a dismissive gesture. "You gained nothing from his death. And that fact can be shown through quite basic economic analysis. So you see, you haven't anything to worry about."

Gregory Shepherd looked simultaneously relieved and puzzled.

"Well, Gregory, I shall have to be on my way back to London," Herbert Grundy tooted as he reappeared from the small passageway.

"Couldn't find anything?"

"It was Marshall I had my heart set on," he said in an affected voice, while clasping his hands to his breast. "If I can't have Marshall, I shan't have anything at all."

Shepherd smiled at his customer's mimicry. Grundy was a study in contradictions, an androgynous soul if there ever was one.

"Hold on a moment. I just remembered something. Your luck may have changed." Shepherd slipped behind the beige curtain and into the room from which Spearman had been evicted. A moment later Shepherd reappeared, holding a hefty-looking tome.

"I was right. You *are* in luck! Some time ago, I acquired a first edition of the *Principles*. It was during a hectic period, when we were doing some remodeling, and I placed it out of harm's way in the back of the store. Then I forgot about it. Until a few minutes ago, anyway. If you still want it, it's yours. A hundred and five pounds."

A surprised Grundy eyed Shepherd suspiciously for a moment, then reached for his checkbook while an amused Henry Spearman watched the proceedings with interest.

Chapter 17:
Much Ado about Maps

As the clock struck the hour, Henry Spearman strolled through the big double gate and under a massive archway that served as the main entrance to Bishop's College. He emerged onto a cobblestone walk. In the distance he could see a quadrangle of green grass flanked by solid three-story structures that served as living quarters for the undergraduates and some of the unmarried dons.

At the back end of the courtyard, straight-on, stood the College chapel. Across the square just to the right was the dining hall, a large, thick-walled stone building of classical architecture. That's where Hart's body was found, Spearman thought to himself.

Spearman turned left through the arch, walked under a portico, and faced the doors of the porter's lodge. The economist paused before entering. But he thought that the lodge would have information helpful to him for the afternoon's journey.

It was a busy place. Milling about were undergraduates, a few in gowns, some in college blazers, others in nondescript attire, who had dropped in to check for messages and mail or simply to exchange pleasantries and gossip with other students.

Laid out upon a narrow oak counter that ran the length of the room were small stacks of circulars, notices, and assorted papers of varying shapes, sizes, and colors. In the booth behind the counter were two men in formal black suits. The black bowlers, which they always wore when they stepped outside the lodge,

115

were on a hatrack by their side. One of the two men was the senior porter, the other his assistant.

Spearman observed the senior porter with some curiosity. He knew that, in spite of his title, a senior porter is more likely to be seen carrying the college keys then lugging someone's suitcase. But the economist also knew that the senior porter carried around in his head a veritable storehouse of information.

"Can I help you, sir?" The assistant porter, Tom Pickett, had noticed that the diminutive stranger seemed a bit lost.

"Possibly. I was wondering if you might have maps of Cambridge here?"

"No maps for sale here, sir," Pickett responded. "Try down the street at McCutchen's." Pickett saw the look of disappointment on the face of the newcomer.

"I must be misinformed. I understood I could get maps here."

"And who led you to believe that, sir?"

"Professor Jared McDonald. He told me if I ever needed directions or information about Cambridge, just stop in a porter's lodge and ask."

"Oh, are you an acquaintance of Professor McDonald's?"

"Yes, we're friends. My wife and I are staying at his home."

"Oh, I see, sir. That's a different matter. We aren't permitted to give maps out to every tourist who stops by and asks. The bursar once told all the porters that if we gave a map to everyone who asked, it would use up the College's whole endowment! That's how the bursar put it. There's *that* many tourists in Cambridge. More each year, it seems. And most of 'em come with no sense of where anything is."

"Maybe you should sell maps," Spearman suggested to Mr. Pickett, with a grin. "Then you could *add* to the College's endowment. Bishop's bursar wouldn't mind that, I'll bet."

"Oh, we couldn't do that, sir. We couldn't sell maps. Not here at the lodge."

"Why is that?" Spearman asked, a look of puzzlement on his face.

"Wouldn't be proper, sir. Not proper at all." Tom Pickett thought about how to explain to the lodge's visitor what to him seemed like such a basic point.

"Bishop's is a college," he said. "Not a business. Besides, what would the people at McCutchen's think?"

"Another way of looking at it," Spearman replied, "is to ask what the tourists might prefer? To purchase a map here, where they've chosen to stop, or be sent somewhere else? I suspect they would pay for the privilege of not having to go elsewhere."

Warren Thorne had been listening to the conversation between his colleague and Henry Spearman, while filing some mail. He stepped over to the counter next to his junior associate and said, "Don't get Mr. Pickett wrong, sir. The College's always believed that tourists were guests in Cambridge. But just like your guests at home, you don't give them everything they want. Me and Mr. Pickett here, we try to help with directions if we have time.

"Now, in your case, that's different, sir. Seeing as how you know Dr. McDonald." Thorne reached under the counter.

"We always keep a large map of the whole area at the lodge," he continued. "Sometimes we get questions where we need a big map." Thorne showed Spearman a document which, unfolded, would have covered most of the counter at the lodge.

"Then we've got these." Thorne pulled out a stack of smaller maps, which were sheets of paper only folded twice. The smaller maps showed just the streets and lanes in the University area of Cambridge, the University's colleges, and the most notable tourist sites.

"We keep a bunch of these maps—walking maps, I call them— and I can give you one of them. Now if you want to look for something on the large map, we can spread it out right here, sir. But if the little map suits you, you can take one with you. Gift of the College," Thorne said.

"You're very kind," Spearman replied. "I'll tell you what. I'll borrow a small map for now, and simply take it over here to study it a bit." Spearman gestured to a shelf that ran along the opposite wall. "I'm starting to get a sense of where I am. If it seems helpful, I won't hesitate to accept your offer to take the map with me. I've seen so many people standing on the streets of Cambridge trying to unfold and read a map that I won't be embarrassed to join them," he chuckled.

Henry took the map to the shelf, where three students were

going through their mail and messages. He unfolded the document and began to study it.

Walking around Cambridge had made many of the major streets familiar to him. But he was a bit concerned about the roads he had not walked or ridden on with Jared and that he would need to travel that afternoon when he and Pidge went to visit Steve Pipes for their tour of Grantchester. Spearman was relieved to see it was not a great distance from Jared's house to the road that would take them out of town to the little village they wanted to explore.

As he stood in the porter's lodge engaged in this activity, Spearman thought to himself about the similarity between a map and an economic theory. At Harvard, he often encountered students new to economics who complained at what they took to be the impracticality of economic analysis. "Give me the facts," he remembered one student saying to him. "Not just theory."

In such situations, Spearman would cite the ordinary road map as a case in point. Standing that afternoon in the porter's lodge, he wondered if perhaps he should show an actual map, like the one before him, to illustrate his point.

"A map," he would tell the student, "would be useless if it covered *every* detail. Imagine a map that was drawn on a one-to-one scale. It would be very unwieldy, wouldn't it?" he would kid the student. "By the time you got it unfolded, it would cover the entire area you wanted to learn about."

"No," he would say, "the *only* way a map is useful is if it leaves out major parts of reality. And it's the same with economic theory. Theory is useful only if it abstracts away from complex reality just as a map does."

Spearman's musings were interrupted by a conversation on the other side of the porter's lodge at the lodger's main counter. He strained to hear a discussion between Thorne and a delinquent undergraduate who had been summoned before him. The senior porter was observing the appropriate formalities. Politely, but firmly, he was dressing a young man down.

"I regret to say that your conduct with regard to your bedder was quite improper. You could have done her serious physical harm. It would not be tolerated in any Cambridge college and most definitely will not be tolerated at Bishop's. Make no mistake about it. If I hear of such behavior again, I shall report your offense to the Master. I can assure you, sir, you would not want that to happen. I've seen young men sent down for less. I shall expect you to send a written apology to Mrs. Tolmie. She should receive it by the end of the week.''

The tall, square-faced undergraduate in khakis and blazer stood rigidly straight throughout the ordeal. He reddened slightly but perceptibly, then asked, ''Is that all, sir?''

''That is all, Mr. Wool. Good day.''

Spearman listened in fascinated admiration. For in such a matter the senior porter is in a delicate situation. Although he has the moral weight of authority behind him, he must play a mixed role, both inferior and superior to the student. With thirty-five years of experience behind him, Warren Thorne carried it off with aplomb.

Spearman was enjoying the ambience of the porter's lodge and so he purposely dawdled over his map. Students, dons and visitors came and went. Periodically Thorne would disburse mail, messages, and packages.

''Mr. Harrison, a message from Downing, sir. It was delivered about an hour ago.''

''Mr. Lyons, there's some post for you here.''

''Dr. Merrifield, a large package came for you, sir. It's rather a load. I can have Pickett bring it to your rooms, if you like.''

''Mr. Percival, your tutor, Mr. Tuckett, asked me to tell you he regrets he'll be unable to meet with you this afternoon. He'll try to contact you later this week to rearrange.''

Warren Throne took pride in his ability to remember the faces of the Fellows and undergraduates at Bishop's. The senior porter had learned to associate a distinctive physical feature of each person's physiognomy with the sound of his name. It had become something of a mental game for him. Thus, for example, the hirsute Mr. Harrison became, in Thorne's mind, 'hairy son'. As soon as he spotted the young man anyplace, the image of a hairy son came into Thorne's head. With lightning speed, 'hairy son' was transformed into 'Harrison'. Thorne found that, with sufficient ingenuity on his part, the method worked in every case.

Henry Spearman watched the senior porter's performance with considerable amazement not unmixed with envy. It took Spearman half a semester to learn the names of his students in any class with an enrollment larger than ten. This could cause some slight embarrassment. When he returned midterm examination papers he had difficulty recognizing the student who belonged to the name on the blue book.

Before exiting the porter's lodge Spearman congratulated Thorne on his remarkable memory. The senior porter nodded his head appreciatively and, with a serious demeanor, responded to Spearman's compliment.

"I'd put it down to experience, sir. I've been on the job thirty-five years now. After awhile you get the hang of it and it gets easier. For some it comes natural. Pickett here, for instance, puts the name and the face together just like that." Thorne snapped his fingers to accompany his example. "But I have to work at it. And the older I get, the harder it gets.

"For me, faces come easier now than names. I mean, I never forget a face. However long ago it was I met someone, I'll remember his face. Sometimes a Bishop's man from as far back as twenty years will visit the College and I'll remember him. I mayn't be able to get the name, but I'll know *him*, however much he's aged. Some features always remain in a face, no matter how many years it's got on it. The ears, for example. They don't show aging so clear. And there's a look about the eyes that stays the same, too.

"Just a few evenings ago I saw someone come through the gate into the court. I said to myself, 'I know that person from somewhere. It was a long time ago, and I can't place who it is.' And when something like that happens, it gnaws at me and gnaws at me until, suddenly, I remember: the face gets matched with a name, and then I know. After that, I'll usually remember all sorts of other things. It hasn't happened yet, but eventually I'll remember who it was I saw in the court that night. Of course, if it's something best forgotten, I won't mention a thing. 'Let sleeping dogs lie' is what I say."

Listening to Thorne describe his remarkable talent to observe and remember, Spearman began to reflect on Thring's appraisal of Cambridge porters. They know everything, good and evil, that takes place within their college's walls. Unlike the three monkeys, they hear evil and see evil. But, like their wise simian counterparts, they speak no evil. They are too discreet for that.

Spearman realized that even if a senior porter had heard or seen the evil by some person or persons plotting to dispatch Morris Fain through the expedient of a well-aimed dumbbell, he would not speak to an outsider like Henry Spearman about it.

Take Warren Thorne, for instance. Spearman was convinced that if Warren Thorne had been the senior porter at St. John's, he would know a great deal more than the police, or anyone else, about what really happened to cause a dumbbell to smash into the punt transporting Morris Fain.

On the other hand, Thring had admitted the possibility, unlikely though it was, that someone, an extremely clever someone, might outwit a porter, even one as perceptive as Warren Thorne.

As Spearman was preparing to exit the porter's lodge at Bishop's, Mr. Pickett spoke out to him. "It isn't just maps, sir, that the tourists want. You'd be surprised how many of 'em come in asking to use the loo. They think the porter's lodge is a public loo. But it's not that at all. It's a porter's lodge. So if we started selling maps, even at profit, we'd have more people asking to use the facilities."

"Interesting idea," Spearman said. "Perhaps there's another opportunity to add to the endowment at Bishop's College."

"Oh, we couldn't to that, sir. You can't charge people to use a loo."

Chapter 18:
Grantchester's Miss Marple

The roundabouts were the worst.

Americans who have never driven in England think traveling on the left side of the road would be difficult to learn, especially after years of reacting to traffic patterns that are just the opposite. The Spearmans found driving on the left side of the road could be accomplished by unremitting concentration on keeping their car in what instinctively seemed to be the wrong lane. Approaching vehicles on the right served as a constant reminder to stay left.

But the roundabouts, where traffic proceeded in a circle around an island, with cars peeling off at different roads along the perimeter, were a different matter. The English believed their roundabouts facilitated travel because stoplights were eliminated and therefore traffic purportedly could keep moving. This may be true for experienced drivers, but not for newcomers.

What the Spearmans found counter-intuitive, after years of left-hand turns being the more difficult to make in the States, was the reversal of one's expectations in England. It was a *right* hand turn that required intense concentration and dexterity. The car had to travel two hundred and seventy degrees, three-quarters of a full circle, around the center island just to turn right.

Their first time out, the Spearmans circled two roundabouts more than once before they discovered the exit for the road they wanted. An automobile going round and round was a sure sign of a driver new to English roads.

Pidge and Henry Spearman had rented an automobile during this visit to England, a white, two–door Vauxhall Viva compact. In the States, Henry drove a boxy, full-sized sedan. Given the narrow English roads, he was glad for the downsized motorcar he and Pidge had selected. Jared McDonald had offered the Spearmans his own car, but Henry had declined, in part not to inconvenience his friend, in part because he was uncertain of its insurance status while he or Pidge was driving it.

The Spearmans' travel objective this afternoon was a very modest one: to make their way out of Cambridge's busy streets and go two miles south-southwest to the nearby village of Grantchester, where Steve Pipes had offered to show them around. Pipes had kidded them that they should rent a punt and pole their way to Grantchester, since the Spearmans had had the opportunity to observe how it was done during their time with him the day before. The Spearmans demurred. Because both enjoyed walking, Pidge and Henry had considered taking the footpath that joined Cambridge and Grantchester, but they decided against that alternative on account of the time and because they were told the walkway did not always follow the Cam.

"I think Jared said we should see a sign about here," Pidge volunteered to her husband. She served as an extra set of eyes for her husband in the car, which he appreciated. Because of his small stature, Henry Spearman did not have the unobstructed view of the road that a taller driver enjoyed. At home, much of his driving was done looking beneath the top half of the steering wheel and just over the dashboard. On the smaller Vauxhall, his size seemed to make it harder for him to view the road because the steering wheel often was in the line of his vision.

"There's the sign—take a left here, Henry. This should take us straight to Grantchester." Spearman was relieved to hear that only a left turn was required. He steered the car along the outer edge of the roundabout and veered off at his first option.

In a short time they had entered the village and soon had found the driveway to Mrs. Saltmarsh's home. There was another car in the driveway, but Henry saw there was room to pull in alongside it.

"Oh, good, there's Steve Pipes now," Pidge observed, as she saw their young guide from yesterday bounding down the stone steps at the front door of the house. Dressed in American-style jeans and a dark blue cotton turtleneck, Pipes could have passed for a graduate student at an American university.

"This is the place," Pipes called out. "I see you found it—I trust without difficulty."

"No problem getting here. It's going back that concerns me. All the left turns will become right ones. I think that follows, doesn't it?"

Pipes was uncomprehending. He looked askance at Spearman, but responded as though he had not heard the question. "I can't introduce you to my landlady, Mrs. Saltmarsh, right now. She's popped over to the shop for some cream. But she'll be back and wants you to have some tea with her. She thinks I wouldn't know how to serve you myself, and she's opposed—on principle so far as I can make out—to people going out for afternoon tea. So I told her I'd show you around the village, and when we return, I'll introduce you. I hope you can stay for some tea. My landlady's a dear, and tea won't detain you long."

"We would enjoy that," Pidge said for the both of them. "She doesn't have to go to the trouble, though. We're grateful just to have the tour. You're kind to take the time. You already must have your fill of tourists, just from your job."

"Oh, Steven! Will I be able to get my car out okay?" A woman's voice called out from an upstairs window.

"Yes, you're not blocked in. Come down and let me introduce you to my guests," Steve called back. In less than two minutes time the Spearmans noticed a young woman starting towards them across the yard. She was wearing a beige linen mini-skirt and a white cotton blouse. Her long blond hair hung straight down to her waist. As she came closer, Pidge noticed her impeccable facial complexion enhanced by a brown velvet dog-collar necklace. Tube bangles adorned her wrists.

"Dolores, these are my American guests I told you about, Professor and Mrs. Spearman. I'm going to show them around the village. By land. Not punt. That'll be a change for me," Pipes said, motioning to his guests. "And this is Dolores Tanner," he continued. "She rents a part of the house too—but she works in London and commutes. So she really does live in two different worlds."

"Is today a vacation day for you?" Pidge Spearman asked, making conversation.

"I'm afraid in my line of work there are many vacation days. I'm an actress. I work mainly in London, though I do some touring, too. At the moment, I'm waiting to hear about a new role I auditioned for," Tanner said awkwardly. "I'm sorry to have bothered you about the car. From my room, I couldn't tell if you were blocking me in or not, and I'm going out a bit later."

"This is a new car for her," Steve said, looking at Dolores kiddingly. "She is very protective of it. I give her about six months for such behavior, and then she'll treat it as most Englishmen do."

"It's *hardly* a new car, Steven, and I'm hardly being protective of it. The fact I let you drive it yesterday should be proof of that. If I had bought a new Jaguar, then you'd see me as zealous as any yeoman of the guard. I'd probably keep a doberman chained out there. But I think I've been quite reasonable about this car. I don't even cover it at night." Dolores acted as if she were peeved, but her smile kept her performance from fooling anyone.

"Do you drive to London?" Pidge asked, imagining to herself the strain such a drive would be for either Henry or herself.

"Oh no, I had been looking for a car just to get me to Cambridge station and back. And some other running about. I bought this one because I thought it would serve that purpose."

"Professor Spearman could tell you precisely why you bought the car, Dolores. I think I told you, he's an economics professor in America."

"That shouldn't be too hard in my case. I just said I bought the car to get to the train station."

"No, I mean the real reason, the theoretically correct reason, based on your utility function and all that," Pipes replied, as if trying to tease Henry Spearman into the conversation.

"All I can say about the economics is I paid plenty. But it seemed to be the best buy for me," Dolores replied, looking with appreciation at her recent acquisition.

"I tried to get her to buy an almost identical car for the same price from a friend of mine who had one in really good condition. I even drove it by for her to see. But what does she do? Ignores me and goes off and buys this one from a dealer instead," Pipes said to the Spearmans, pointing his thumb at his friend. Half turning to Dolores, he smiled and continued. "Theater people are more impulsive than the rest of us; they really are."

"Your method of choosing may not let you down this time," Henry Spearman said to the actress. "In the United States, there's a sales pitch used car dealers are said to employ: 'This car was owned by a little old lady who drove it only to church on Sunday.' This meant the vehicle was supposed to be a very low-risk purchase, if the story of the car's provenance was true. I would imagine the same situation would hold if you knew a car had been owned by the Master of a college who drove it only once a week to a bookstore. That's probably the extent of the wear and tear on this car. It belonged to Nigel Hart."

Pipes and Tanner, as well as Pidge Spearman, all looked surprised. "How do you know that to be the case, Henry?" his wife asked.

"Don't you remember? The night we went to the Hales' and had difficulty finding a place to park? Jared drove us and we ended up in a space right behind this car. Jared pointed it out to us as Nigel Hart's vehicle, mentioning that even college masters have no easy time finding a parking space in Cambridge. I remember noting the car to see if Masters, like a lot of deans in American universities, play down their income level by driving rather modest automobiles. And I remember the yellow decal in the back window. See it there? 'B.C.' Bishop's College, I presume.

"In any event, Miss Tanner, good luck with the car. I'm sure you are safer letting Steve borrow it than me. And I trust Steve is right—we're not blocking you, are we?"

"No, not at all. I probably won't even leave before you do."

"We shall not be long, actually," Henry Spearman replied. "Steve kindly offered to show us around. We're coming back shortly to have some tea with your landlady. Then we must leave. My wife is attending a recital early this evening with our host." Spearman paused, to signal to Pipes that it was best they get on their way.

"We'd be delighted to have you join us on our walk," Pidge added.

"You are both sweet to say that. But I think Steven wants to do the tour. For every question you have about Grantchester, he might have one for you about going to college in the USA.''

Pipes and the Spearmans started off through the scenic village.

Grantchester is old. The village existed before the Domesday Book of 1086. Twentieth-century construction, which had marred so much of Cambridge's ambience, was nil in the village of Grantchester.

''We'll carry on up Church Lane, then turn off to get to the Cam. I want to show you one of the most famous parts of the river that you didn't see yesterday, because we didn't come up this way.''

Pipes took his guests to the pastoral setting now called Byron's Pool. ''He swam here while he was a student at Trinity. You can still see Byron's rooms at the College. But this was where he loved to be.'' Pipes made an expansive gesture encompassing the stunning scene. ''I know you are trying to buy the place where Alfred Marshall got inspired, but people in the village would tell you this is where Byron got inspired.''

''It *is* a beautiful spot, one has to concede that,'' Henry Spearman said. ''But if he could get his work done while swimming and lazing here, then I picked the wrong line of work.''

''Henry, if you spent a day here, you would end up wondering about the value of the land, or the current price of the cattle per hundredweight.''

''Pidge, that's not fair,'' Henry protested to his wife with a smile.

''You see what an economist has to put up with, Steve? Maybe you should reconsider doing graduate work in the field. You'll only be misunderstood, even by the ones you love.''

The walk back to Mrs. Saltmarsh's home gave Henry and Pidge the opportunity to talk with Pipes about educational opportunities at an American university. Henry advised him to enter a mid-tier school at first, where he would have a good chance of gaining financial support. Then, if he excelled, use his record to gain entry to the doctoral program of a top-tier school.

''I don't know, Dr. Spearman. Sometimes I wonder if I've got what it takes to go to university. I feel I've got enough to do as it is. I try to keep reading in economics. I know I should do that just about every day. But I have my job on the river; that takes time. And I like to spend some time with my landlady." Steve pointed out Mrs. Saltmarsh's home as they approached it. "She's very sweet, and I think she's a bit lonely too. My family lives in Somerset and I want to see as much of them as I can. Then, I like to play a bit of football, too. I feel guilty if I spend time on football, but it keeps me fit."

"Why feel guilty?" Spearman asked. "All that you say simply tells me that you are optimizing. You know that from your economics: we're always making trade-offs just like you describe. A little bit more of this activity means a little bit less of that. All this moves us toward an equilibrium. There's nothing wrong with your optimizing. And nothing surprising, either."

As they crossed the lawn of Mrs. Saltmarsh's yard, Pipes recognized Mrs. Saltmarsh's voice calling to them from the back porch.

"You might as well come in the back way. I try to keep a proper sitting room, but it seems everyone who visits ends up in the back of the house, or in the kitchen. So come on and use the back door. But we'll have our tea in the sitting room—if nobody minds, that is."

Steve Pipes introduced Mrs. Saltmarsh to his guests, who nodded graciously to Pipes's landlady. Steve had explained earlier to Pidge and Henry how Mrs. Saltmarsh always put on a bold front with people, but that deep down, she was a very shy person, especially with those she considered to be of a higher social class than herself.

"Steve tells me you're here to buy a house," Mrs. Saltmarsh said after everyone was seated, cups of steaming tea on a coffee table before them.

"We do have a house in mind, but not for ourselves, as Steve probably told you. We want to acquire a house that was occupied for many years by a prominent Cambridge economist; we want to develop it for educational purposes," Henry Spearman explained.

Mrs. Saltmarsh passed her guests a silver-plated tray that held containers of orange marmalade and preserves. "This'll dress up the crumpets a bit. I know Americans don't always like marmalade, but this kind isn't bitter. But if you'd rather, there's some nice strawberry jam I made myself. The marmalade's shop-bought. But I can vouch for the jam." Both Spearmans chose the jam.

"I took the Spearmans all around Grantchester, mum, and then we talked about my going to college," Pipes volunteered, helping himself to milk for his tea.

"Steve's a bright boy," Mrs. Saltmarsh said. "I can tell you that. I never was one for maths. But he can balance my checkbook in a lick. Doing all the calculations in his head, mind you. And it comes out right. Right down to the last penny. He'll do you credit as a student. Not that I want him to go. You get a good lodger and you hate to see him leave. Anybody who takes in lodgers will tell you that. Losing Steve will be like losing one of the family."

"I'm not about to leave, mum. I've got things to tend to here. Professor Spearman simply talked to me about some of the possible alternatives in America."

"If you get your house, Professor, couldn't Steve just study there?" Mrs. Saltmarsh's face was lined and wrinkled as she asked her hopeful question.

"I'm afraid not," Spearman replied, placing his half-consumed crumpet on his plate. He took a sip of tea. "We envision the house being for established young economists, not students. Perhaps someday, when Steve has begun to make a reputation for himself, he could come back. I know from what he has told me that Steve wouldn't forget you if he were away. If he came back, I suspect he would prefer to live here with you anyway, rather than on Madingley.

"In any event, we don't have the house finally pinned down as yet. As you probably know, it took a very unfortunate event even to make the place an option for us again."

"We all know about Dr. Hart's death, even the folks in Grantchester. Before the man could even get in the house, he ends up dead in a box. I'm superstitious about such things. If life's going well for you, best stay put," Mrs. Saltmarsh said gravely.

She poured herself a tad more tea and invited her guests to more. "You wouldn't get me to move from here, just to be on Madingley Road. I've told Steve, if they get me out of this house, it will be in a hearse. Not a day before. Poor man. Not that I knew him, of course. But everyone I know thinks it's dreadful the police can't find who did it. There's no ending the man's shame if they don't find who killed him. I can remember when the police solved crimes. And they were quick about it too. Now they just investigate them.''

"Oh, I suspect the killer will be caught," Pidge Spearman volunteered. But then a look of uncertainty crossed her face. "Or is that an American prejudice? The British police have such a remarkable reputation—in America, at least. We believe Scotland Yard always solves the crime.''

"That happens in the films and on TV," Mrs. Saltmarsh replied quickly. "But here, I think the police are on the wrong track. They won't solve it the way they're going about it, you wait and see. And Mr. Taggart agrees with me on that. He's the baker on Church Lane.''

"Mum has a theory of who killed Nigel Hart," Pipes explained. "She's sure she's right.''

"And what is your theory, Mrs. Saltmarsh?" Henry asked with some curiosity.

"It's the College staff, that's who it'll be. The police are looking all around at other dons and even merchants. That's what we hear. I can't say for sure about the merchants. But it was no don. We've some of them in Grantchester. They don't have the heart for that kind of thing. Neither would the staff a while back, mind you. A full bedder or porter would never think of harmin' their College Master. But the young ones today are different. They don't appreciate having a steady job; they don't show a proper respect. They're harder. Dress them down and they'll get back at you. Even when they need the dressing down. So, it's the staff that did it. At least that's my theory. But then I don't expect no one to pay much attention to an old woman.''

"Don't sell yourself short, Mrs. Saltmarsh," Pidge Spearman intervened, placing her hand upon the woman's arm. "To Americans, the most famous amateur sleuth in England is a woman about your age. The local police learned the hard way not to ignore Miss Jane Marple's intuition. They may learn not to ignore your theory about the murder of Dr. Hart.''

Flattered by the comparison, Mrs. Saltmarsh thought to herself how much she was enjoying her American guests.

Chapter 19:
Adverse Selection

Pidge Spearman turned the knob on the guest room door and walked into darkness. With her right hand she groped along the wall in the area where she thought the light switch might be. Frustration. Then, as her eyes adjusted to the dimness, Pidge made out the floor lamp to the left of the entrance.

She pulled the small chain dangling from the socket. To her astonishment, she was not alone in the room. Her husband, oblivious to the presence of his wife, was sitting on the bench, stock-still, his elbow on the desktop, his chin resting in the palm of his hand.

"Henry, you startled me! What are you doing sitting in the dark?"

"It wasn't dark when I sat down. I'm afraid I lost track of the time. What time *is* it?" He glanced at his watch hurriedly.

"About eight-thirty. Jared and I just got back from the recital. Have you been here all along?" Pidge crossed the room and drew the drapes.

Spearman pushed his glasses up on his forehead and rubbed his eyes. There were deep lines of weariness on his face.

Half turning his head, he looked at his wife quizzically. "Did your mother ever buy the life insurance policy we talked about?"

The unexpected question surprised Pidge until she realized that her husband was in one of his moods. She smiled at him indulgently.

133

"You go first. Answer my questions and then I'll answer yours." She looked playfully at her husband.

With a slight smile, Spearman answered, "Pidge, I have a confession to make. It's a familiar one. I'm afraid you've heard it many times since you married me. I was so lost in my thoughts that I did not quite catch your question."

"Well, there were two of them really. But they're connected. I wondered what you were doing sitting in the dark. And then I wanted to know whether you've been here in the room ever since I left. Your answer—not entirely responsive, I think you'll agree— was whether my mother bought an insurance policy."

"What I've been doing, I've been sitting here ever since you left, thinking about what happened today. All the different events. Trying to piece them together." His face took on an animated expression. "I found myself pacing back and forth in our room. And then at some point, I guess it was just after dark, I sat down at the desk to get a new angle on my thoughts. The next thing I knew a light went on."

"That's when I came in. I turned on the lamp."

"No, before that. Suddenly it became clear to me that I must tell the police to question Dolores Tanner. At that point, I was puzzled about how I was going to approach the authorities. I'd have felt awkward enough doing that in the States. Here, I know even less about police procedures. In any event, it must have been about then that you came back and turned on the lamp. I had just been thinking how I was going to explain my conclusion to the police. Then I remembered our discussion of your mother's insurance policy." His words seemed to tumble over themselves.

"I think she did buy the insurance policy. I never did check to be sure. But so what? How does that connect with Dolores Tanner?"

"It connects because your mother's not a motorcycle racer or a stunt pilot. She's a careful driver; she watches what she eats; she never drinks too much; she has a good doctor. She knows all these things, but the insurance company doesn't. Or at least they don't know them as well as she does. She has more information about herself than they do. She's a good risk, but they don't know just how good a risk she is."

Spearman rose from his seat and walked to the window, parted the drapes slightly and peered out into the night. Then he turned toward Pidge and leaned back against the windowsill.

"Insurance companies don't know for sure who the bad risks are either. But the people who are bad risks know. Insurance would be a good deal for them. Insurance companies, to survive financially, have to charge higher premiums for everyone. That makes insurance less attractive to people like your mother. So there's a process of adverse selection. The outcome is inefficient. It could happen that only the worst risks get insured, everyone else having been driven out of the market."

"So?" Pidge still had puzzled look on her face.

Spearman drew a sharp breath. "So that's how I'll get the police to understand why they need to pay a visit to Dolores Tanner," he said drily.

Henry Spearman pushed himself away from the window ledge and began to make his way purposefully to the hall telephone. Beneath the telephone table, he found a dog-eared Cambridge directory. Quickly, he located the number of the police and began dialing.

"Good evening. My name is Henry Spearman. I'm calling from the home of Professor Jared McDonald near Jesus Green. I'd like to speak to the detective assigned to the case of Nigel Hart. Can you connect me with that person?"

"That would be Lieutenant Forbush. I believe he's still here. You said your name is Spearmint?"

"Spearman. Henry Spearman."

"Oh, Spearman? And this is about the Hart case? . . . Yes, I have it down, sir. . . . And what did you say your name was? . . . Oh, yes, sorry sir. . . . Spearman. . . . One moment, please."

Lieutenant Donald Forbush was second in command among the detectives on the police force of the city of Cambridge. He and his superior officer shared the duty of investigating the Nigel Hart murder. Homicides were extremely rare in England's East Anglia region. Forbush and his colleague's total combined experience with this crime was three. Their batting average was a very respectable .667.

"Forbush here. I understand you're calling about the Hart matter. How can I help you?"

Spearman hesitated before answering. His voice sounded unnatural and stiff. "I believe I can tell you who murdered Nigel Hart."

"Right, sir. And who might that man be?" Forbush sounded skeptical.

"Actually, it's a woman."

Now it was Forbush's turn to hesitate. "Oh, I see, sir. And can you give me her name?"

"Yes, I can. I've met her. Her name is Dolores Tanner." Henry Spearman proceeded to explain the theory behind his conclusion that the actress had killed the Master of Bishop's College. Detective Forbush listened patiently to the entire explanation and then asked Henry Spearman to repeat it.

"I'm not sure I understand all you've said, sir. But I doubt if there's enough there to warrant an arrest."

"Detective Forbush, all I ask of you is that you call on Miss Tanner tomorrow and ask her where she was at the time of Nigel Hart's death. Then ask her about her purchase of Nigel Hart's car. I recommend that you order a search of the vehicle. I have no doubt that the knife that killed Nigel Hart was once inside the car and there may be bloodstains to prove this. You have your way of finding the truth; I have mine."

"I'm willing to go along with you this far," Forbush responded. "I'll take a chance you may be right. How about this, Professor Spearman? You come with me to Grantchester tomorrow morning. We'll both observe how Miss Tanner responds to your theory when it is presented to her directly."

Spearman was pleased with the detective's reaction. He could understand the tentative response of Forbush to his analysis. Spearman's economic reasoning was unlikely to convince a non-econmist. Yet it seemed that Forbush vaguely understood, even if he could not follow, all the subtleties of a problem involving asymmetric information. At least Forbush thought it conceivable Spearman was right. In this instance, Spearman *knew* he was right.

Chapter 20:
The One in the Many, the Many in the One

He was wrong. Forbush estimated Miss Tanner had been dead for only a short time. Rigor mortis had not set in. There was some stiffness in her neck, but rigor was not yet established in her body's larger muscles. A single red smudge above her left eye revealed the point where a bullet had entered her skull. Her head was cocked to the side against the cushion of the chair where the two men found her seated. Her eyes had the glassy stare of the dead.

To Spearman, the sitting room appeared undisturbed. It was as he had remembered it from his visit with Steve Pipes. A tea setting was on the table next to the chair. Spearman touched the side of the teapot. The water had cooled. He walked to the kitchen.

The room was tidy and clean, in contrast to the buzzing confusion Spearman felt. Everything he knew about asymmetric information theory had convinced him Tanner had murdered Hart. But that she should meet the same fate herself some two weeks later seemed too coincidental for his orderly mind to accept easily. Two murders in two weeks committed by two different people? Possible. Certainly not probable.

A world of possibilities was not Spearman's world. He had been trained to live in a world of probabilities. It was the probabilities that had led him to Miss Tanner as the culprit in Hart's death. Now it seemed that some other reasoning had led someone else to Tanner. A murderer murdering another murderer? Why? There had to be a reason. Spearman could not make sense of it. Surely Hart's murderer had struck again. This time the victim was Tanner. How odd that Spearman should have thought Tanner was the killer when all along the real killer had selected her as the next victim.

Detective Forbush entered the kitchen, putting Spearman's puzzlement into abeyance. "I've had a look in the other rooms. As I expected, there's no one there. Mrs. Saltmarsh must be out. That lad you know—Peeps is it?—isn't here either."

"The boy's name is Pipes, Steven Pipes."

"It was probably someone she knew," Forbush said. "There is no sign of forced entry. Not even a sign of a struggle. It appears she was about to serve tea to her killer."

At this juncture, Forbush made a decision. "I'm going to call to have Pipes brought in for questioning immediately. If he's still within a hundred miles of here. I also need to get hold of the coroner." He left the kitchen to search for a telephone.

Spearman was left alone. He felt that his powers of deduction had failed him. There remained the power of induction. Induction was not his forte as a way of arriving at the truth. He was a theorist, most at home with constructing hypotheses built on basic axioms of human behavior. This method had carried him far. It permitted him to abstract from a single instance to encompass the general case. From the particular to the general. What Alfred Marshall called the ability to find "the many in the one." That is what Spearman did best.

Spearman had no objection to the work of his economist colleagues who were number crunchers, who searched for "the one in the many." An empiricist would ask whether a pattern could be discovered in the welter of seemingly unrelated stimuli that greet the senses? Can an infinite number of facts in some way add up to a finite truth? Marshall believed a great economist could see the one in the many *and* the many in the one. Not having found the many in the one, Spearman decided to search Mrs. Saltmarsh's home for the one in the many.

The method of induction offered Spearman no guidance as to where to begin his search. Since he was in the kitchen, he started there. The cupboards above the counter and sink were only partially full of dishes, reflecting, Spearman thought, Mrs. Saltmarsh's modest means and lack of family. Under the sink were cleaning materials, many of the containers having labels with brand names Spearman recognized from the United States. The kitchen drawers had the usual paraphernalia: flatware, kitchen knives, ladles, a spatula, and other items a person would use for baking and serving.

Spearman left the kitchen and began his inspection of the sitting room. It was strange how little eeriness he felt looking through a room's furnishings in the presence of a corpse. Forbush's business-like approach to death had affected Spearman.

Spearman noticed a stairway leading to the upper floor, where he thought that Steve Pipes and Dolores Tanner probably had their rooms. When the Spearmans had first encountered Miss Tanner, she had hollered to them from an upstairs window. Henry Spearman made his way up the wooden staircase and turned down a short hallway leading into a bedroom at the front of the house. The door was partially open. Spearman peered inside and saw a wall decorated with posters from theatrical productions. He walked inside.

At first, he studied the posters. On the desk beneath advertisements, he saw a small record player. Spearman opened it and then pawed through about thirty records that sat vertically alongside the phonograph. Recordings of original cast albums from various musical productions dominated the collection.

Next Spearman looked at the small framed pictures over the bed. There were four of them, each one a Victorian print of a different English flower with its identity given in Latin. Spearman had seen such prints in the secondhand bookstores and print shops around Cambridge. He noted there were no pictures of family or friends anywhere to be seen. He walked to the mantelpiece over the fireplace at the back of the room, upon which an assortment of cosmetics and makeup was arrayed.

There was a corner table to the left of the window. Spearman turned his attention to the material spread out on its top. He leafed through an assortment of playbills for various productions in which, he noticed, Dolores Tanner had made an appearance. She had never had a leading role, but her name was listed in the cast for each of the programs Spearman examined. He also observed that Dolores Tanner's acting experience was not confined to England. She had traveled with troupes giving performances in Canada and the United States. She had been part of productions in such cities as Toronto, Chicago, Detroit, St. Louis, and Milwaukee.

"The coroner will be here shortly." Henry Spearman was interrupted by the voice of Donald Forbush, who had entered the room behind him. "What are you doing, Professor Spearman? Everything must be left as we found it. You aren't to move anything. If you'll come downstairs with me, I'd like to ask you a few questions."

The two men made their way out of the bedroom and back to the living room, where Miss Tanner's body had been found. The detective asked the economist to be seated on the couch that faced the deceased.

"Professor Spearman, before the coroner and the chaps from the lab arrive, I'd like a word with you, if you don't mind."

"Not at all."

"Good. Now, as I understand our conversation last evening, you were quite convinced that Miss Tanner was the murderer of Dr. Hart. Is that correct?"

"Absolutely."

"Now, when we agreed to visit the deceased in Grantchester, you were anticipating that we would question Miss Tanner about her purchase of Hart's car. Is that so?"

"Yes. That was my understanding."

"If that's the case, you were assuming all along that we would arrive here this morning and find Miss Tanner alive, not dead. Am I right there?"

"Yes, obviously there'd have been no need to drive out here to question a dead person."

"So your position is that while you knew Miss Tanner stabbed Hart to death, you did not know that she herself would be shot to death while having tea."

"Right on all counts. I did not know she would be shot. I did not know she would be dead. I did not even know she would be having tea."

"Professor Spearman, have you been to this house before?"

"Yes, as I told you on the phone last night, I was here yesterday with my wife. Mr. Pipes had agreed to show us Grantchester. That was the occasion for my meeting Miss Tanner in the first place."

"But you did make your way out here on your own, I assume? You just told me you drove to Grantchester yesterday."

"Yes, I did. But I needed some assistance from a map."

"Can anyone else account for your whereabouts this morning? Before we came out here together, I mean?"

"Yes," Henry Spearman replied, looking up at Forbush. "My wife. And Professor McDonald."

"I see. And I assume, then, you would say you were not in Grantchester earlier this morning?"

"No. As I told you earlier, I was here yesterday. And not again until I rode here with you."

"Then let me ask you this, Professor Spearman. Should it strike me as odd that you would identify Miss Tanner as a murderer, ring me up urging me to interrogate her, and then we find the young woman you claim to be a murderer herself murdered?"

"Yes, you would find it odd. *I* would find it odd. I should think the only one who would *not* find it odd is the murderer."

Chapter 21:
Warren Thorne Remembers

Henry Spearman was back from Grantchester by late morning. A small group of Fellows at Trinity college earlier had invited him to lunch, and it was with reluctance that he honored the commitment. The Grantchester shock had not yet worn off, and he found it difficult to carry on a conversation with the dons.

He was glad when the luncheon was over. Even before the discovery of Dolores Tanner's body, Spearman had thought he would spend part of the afternoon at Heffer's Bookshop in Petty Cury. Visiting scholars from the States often found books there that were published under the imprint of British houses not readily available back home. Losing himself in the stacks at Heffers would give him a welcome respite from the morning's excitement and the noontime obligation to make conversation.

The Spearmans had decided to attend the vespers service to be held later that day in King's College Chapel. Henry Spearman left Heffers and made his way along back streets he had not yet explored to Jared McDonald's home. There he linked up with his wife and gave her a full description of the morning's events.

After a nap and refreshing shower, he saw the first accounts of the Tanner murder on a small television set that Jared McDonald thoughtfully had provided in their bedroom. The news program showed a picture of the actress, pointed out that she had appeared recently in a London production, and announced that the police in Cambridge were following several promising leads.

The Spearmans watched the commentator's account with interest. Murders in England were rare and newsworthy. In England, a murdered person did not have to be famous for the murder to make the news. The murder of anyone had news value.

"Do you think we should try to call Steve Pipes and express our sympathy?" Pidge Spearman asked. "He seemed to be very fond of that girl."

"I tried to call him from Trinity College. Mrs. Saltmarsh told me she had not seen him. I even walked past the punt dock on my way back this afternoon to see if I could find him there. The man in charge told me something very disturbing—that the police were looking for him for questioning, but that nobody seemed to know where he was."

Pidge Spearman gathered her purse and coat, Henry his coat and umbrella, and they made their way to the front door of Mc-Donald's home. "Pidge, on our walk to the chapel, I'd like to stop by the porter's lodge at Bishop's. It's not far out of the way and I never thanked one of the men there for helping us get to Grantchester. I've not been by there today, so I also want to see if any mail or messages might have arrived. Jared usually brings home anything for me that he finds, but I haven't seen him this afternoon."

Pidge Spearman gave her husband a look of assent.

"Good afternoon, sir," Warren Thorne called out when the Spearmans entered the porter's lodge. "I've got some post for you—a couple of letters," he said as he went to the pigeonhole marked "Hold for Visitors." "Not much here, but most of the Fellows seem to think that's good news. Means there aren't many bills, I suppose."

Henry introduced his wife to Bishop's Head Porter and explained how Mr. Thorne had been, more than once, a help in giving directions.

"Well, if I may ask, sir, did you find Grantchester easily? Or did you have problems at the roundabout at the end of Fen Causeway? A lot of our visitors find that to be a tricky one, they do."

"Not only are you a very good trip planner, Mr. Thorne, but my wife is a very good navigator. We made it fine, even at the roundabouts. Actually, I've been to Grantchester twice since I saw you last. Once on the trip we had discussed. This morning, I was escorted by the local police.''

"No! The police? You didn't have a car accident, did you?''

"The circumstances were much stranger than that, I'm afraid. I was with the police when the body of a young woman who was murdered in Grantchester was discovered. You may have seen something on the television about it.''

"Not the TV, not here. The Master would never let us have a TV in the Lodge. I know that to be the case. I asked once. But I certainly read about it in today's newspaper. We can get the paper here. The Master doesn't mind that. But you say you were there?''

"Yes, I had met Dolores Tanner earlier, and I was accompanying a detective who planned to ask her some questions.''

Warren Thorne looked hard at Henry Spearman across the counter of the porter's lodge. "Dolores Tanner you thought she was, did you? That's not who she was when I knew her as a child. Her father was a Fellow here. Nice gentleman, too, he was. He loved that little girl. And if you'd ever seen her, you'd understand why. But he died young and the family moved away. I hadn't seen her for over twenty years. But you remember how I told you once I never forget a face? Names, yes. But not faces. When I saw the picture in today's paper, I put together the face and the name. But it wasn't Tanner. It was the Hesketh girl— grown up now, of course, but that's who it was.''

"Are you sure of that?'' Henry Spearman asked.

"No doubt in my mind. She's the person I told you about. I saw her walking into the College one evening a while back. I couldn't remember her name at that moment—but I was sure I knew her. Then I saw the newspaper. Of course, I said, that's Dr. Hesketh's child. Poor thing, I thought. Died young like her father.''

Chapter 22:
In King's College Chapel

Pidge had insisted that Henry join her for the late afternoon concert at King's College Chapel at Evensong. She now hoped the beauty of the surroundings and the splendor of the music would take Henry's mind off the terrible discovery he had made in Grantchester. For her own part, she did not want to leave the University without experiencing Evensong in Cambridge's famous building.

Henry and Pidge Spearman sat together in the nave beneath the twenty-six huge stained-glass windows of the Chapel. Overhead was a fan-vault looking like a gigantic canopy whose intricate lines suggested the open branches of interlaced palm trees. The day's ebbing light streaming through the colored glass of the west window, the one depicting the Last Judgment, cast rippling shadows into the single vaulted area that formed the interior of the nave. In front of the Spearmans were chancel stalls and a classical screen, the work of a Florentine sculptor of the sixteenth century. To Pidge, who had much more of an interest in architecture than her husband, the internal space within the massive perpendicular structure gave her a feeling of weightlessness. She had read in her guidebook that the fan-vault was the largest in existence and that the building, unlike previous college chapels, was modeled on the cathedral choir.

This evening's sacred music was composed by Mozart. It consisted of five Psalms, each preceded by a hymn and a Magnificat; the College choir was in performance. The combination of music and architecture made Pidge feel she was in the presence of the sublime.

The solemnity of the service fitted perfectly the solemnity of Henry Spearman's mood. The murder of Dolores Tanner was totally unexpected, as was the revelation that Tanner once was named Hesketh. Earlier he had convinced himself that she alone was responsible for the death of Nigel Hart. Her purchase of an automobile about whose provenance and condition she presumably had no information, rather than the purchase of an almost identical car in fine condition about which she had excellent information, had made Spearman realize that Hart's car was wanted for something more valuable to Dolores Tanner than transportation to the train station.

The most likely possibility was that Dolores Tanner hastily had placed the knife she had used to kill Hart somewhere in his automobile. That would explain why the murder weapon never had been found. Purchasing Hart's car allowed her to retrieve the incriminating evidence before it was discovered by another buyer.

But the solution to one puzzle had led to another. The discovery of Dolores Tanner's body at Mrs. Saltmarsh's had pointed toward the likelihood that Tanner had been in league with someone else, someone who did not trust her to keep quiet, someone who wanted to silence her in the event she was caught. That person surely must have conspired with her in the murder of Hart.

Spearman was not given to conspiracy theories to explain every murder. But there are times when a conspiracy is a highly probable explanation of an event. For example, Spearman thought, what if a political leader was shot by an assassin and the next day the assassin, too, was murdered? One would inevitably think it probable the assassin was done in by someone else involved in planning the assassination.

The same logic applied in the case of Tanner. And this reasoning raised new questions. Who had a motive to enter into a conspiracy with Tanner to kill Nigel Hart? Who had a motive to attempt to murder Morris Fain? What did the three of them have in common?

The Lord at thy right hand shall strike through kings in the day of his wrath.

He shall judge among the heathen, he shall fill the places with the dead bodies; The choir in English was chanting the Dixit Dominus of the Vespers. The lyrics exclaimed the irrefutable word of the Lord.

But Henry Spearman was distracted by his own thoughts, and the psalmist's words were absorbed only in the deep well of his unconscious. He felt tense. Lines of fatigue marked his face.

What did Fain, Hart, and Tanner have in common that might link them together in the mind of a diabolical killer?

The fear of the Lord is the beginning of wisdom, sang the tenor and bass in unison. The rest of the choir joined in as the "Confiteor" proclaimed the omnipotence of the Lord's commandments.

But Spearman only half-heard the words and music. He kept rolling over in his mind the crucial question: What did Fain, Hart, and Tanner have in common that would lead someone to want them all dead?

The "Beatus Vir" now rang out its exalted phrases:

Wealth and riches shall be in his house: and his righteousness endureth for ever.

Spearman flinched.

"What's wrong, Henry?" Pidge inquired. She watched her husband with concern. His face had taken on a worried frown.

At first, he did not respond. He had been reminded of something by the choir's words. Spearman removed his thick-lensed glasses, lowered his head, and rubbed his thumb and forefinger across his eyelids until they reached the bridge of his nose which he squeezed tightly. It was an action that sometimes stimulated his memory. But he could not think of what he was reminded of. What were those words?

As if in direct answer to his silent question, the choir repeated the passage:

Wealth and riches shall be in his house. . . .

Suddenly, he smiled and his whole frame relaxed. "The answer is 'Balliol Croft!' " His eyes were twinkling.

"Henry, not so loud." Pidge put her finger to her lips, aware that several spectators nearby had glanced at her husband. "What are you talking about?"

But Henry did not reply. For the first time that evening he was giving rapt attention to the chanting of the oratorio choir. With ecclesiastical solemnity, they were angelically intoning the "Magnificat":

For he that is mighty has done to me great things; and holy is his name.

And his mercy is on them that fear him from generation to generation.

Chapter 23:
Partial Analysis

"You were right, Henry. I'll never again think of prices as unbudgeable. Thring said he was firm at eighteen thousand pounds. Then he writes me that he got five hundred pounds more. But when that deal falls through, he ends up taking seventeen thousand one hundred pounds from us."

Morris Fain said this across the table to his luncheon companion, Henry Spearman.

"You really shouldn't be surprised that you saved nine hundred pounds in getting Balliol Croft. It never fails. Where there is less competition for an asset, the price of that asset falls. Perhaps now the foundation will be able to do some of the extras we had discussed for the use of Balliol Croft." Spearman put down his menu. "Have you given any thought, perhaps, to offering travel allowances to the scholars who will be living there?"

"I really have not given that any consideration," Fain replied.

"Another suggestion I would make is to use the funds to assist the Marshall Library in the assembly and possible publication of Marshall's papers. It would be a fine thing if, right at the outset, the foundation, Balliol Croft, and the Marshall Library had a close working relationship."

"I agree with that, Henry," Fain responded. "We should have a congenial relationship. What we're doing at the house and what they're doing at the Library shouldn't be in conflict."

"Now here's the last suggestion I have. It has nothing to do with academics per se. But I think it might be very fitting. Jared McDonald took me out to visit Alfred Marshall's gravesite at St. Giles' cemetery. I was disappointed at what bad shape it is in. It seems no one has assumed responsibility to keep it up. The grass is full of weeds, the site has stones on it, and the area is in a generally unkempt condition. I don't know what it would cost up front to repair the site. Perhaps it would take only a modest sum to ensure its perpetual care—I think it's called a 'keep neat' contract.

"You also might want to consider adding a headstone. All it now has is a curbstone around the site with Marshall's name and dates. If all this could be done, visitors to Balliol Croft who may want to see Marshall's grave will find a more appropriate memorial, and one more consistent with what we're trying to do with the residence."

"Good idea, Henry. I'll look into that possibility. It might even be that we should consider giving visitors to Balliol Croft information about how they could make a contribution to the enterprise. The foundation is proud, as you know, to be involved in the promotion of Marshall's work. But we can always use more funding."

The Arbor House Hotel, where Fain and Spearman were having lunch, was only a couple of minutes' walk from the city center. The inn was of modern design, which made it unusual in Cambridge. The Blue Boar, where Fain and the Spearmans had stayed on their prior visit, was of much earlier vintage.

The Arbor House was situated in its own grove of trees, which surrounded the hotel on three sides. The front of the building opened to the River Cam. Floral gardens in the front yard separated the hotel from the walkway along the river. From the terrace where they sat, Fain and Spearman could see punters gliding toward Grantchester.

A waiter came to take their order. "I'll have the bookmaker's sandwich on toast, please, and coffee," Fain said.

"That sounds good to me too," Spearman added.

"I'm sorry Pidge could not join us for lunch. I trust she knows how grateful I am—the foundation is, really—for her willingness to come along and assist us in getting Balliol Croft. She knew much more about the structure of a house than either of us did.

"I'm also grateful to you, Henry, for being willing to return on short notice. That was above and beyond the call of any duty, to Marshall or to me. I want you to send me your expenses after you return. I'll see to it that you are reimbursed promptly."

"Pidge is sorry she was occupied. She wanted to see the Fitz-william Museum while it was open today. But I shall tell her what you said. She'll be grateful, I'm sure."

The unusually pleasant lunch made Spearman reluctant to bring up the matter that was most on his mind. It had nothing to do with the success of Balliol Croft, but a more urgent matter concerning Morris Fain's safety.

Spearman leaned across the table towards his host. His voice lowered a tad:

"Morris, that close shave you had—the one in the punt. I've been thinking about that. In fact, Pidge and I took that same ride the day before yesterday, with the same chauffeur you had."

Morris Fain raised his eyebrows as his eyes widened. "Don't tell me you had something similar happen to you?"

"No, no, that's not the point. Our trip was without . . ." Spearman abruptly stopped speaking when their waiter appeared with the order. He kept his silence until the young man was again out of earshot. "As I was saying, our punting expedition was without incident. It's what happened later—yesterday afternoon—that I want to bring to your attention."

Henry Spearman began to recount the events of yesterday afternoon. He explained how his encounter with Steve Pipes had led to his first going to Grantchester. There he had noticed Hart's car and had come to conclude that Hart was murdered by its present owner, a young woman who was a boarder where Steve Pipes lived. Spearman then recounted how he had informed the police, who went with him back to Grantchester, and how there, to the total surprise of both Spearman and the constable who was with him, they had found the body of the young woman. She had been murdered in the house where she and Pipes were boarders.

"The police seem to think Steve Pipes is the culprit, because he can't be found, and the landlady allowed as how her young boarder was infatuated with the girl who was killed. Be that as it may, the killer is still at large, and there's too much coincidence for me not to be uneasy."

"What do you mean by that, Henry?" Fain asked.

"Think about it. Nigel Hart, who has just purchased Balliol Croft, is murdered by a young actress. Her name is Dolores Tanner, and she apparently had no connection to Hart. In short order, Miss Tanner herself is murdered. And just prior to all this, you were almost killed in what appeared to be a freak accident at the very time you were the most likely purchaser of Balliol Croft.

"And here's the part that makes me think your accident was no accident at all. Tanner, too, had a connection to Balliol Croft."

Fain's face took on a look of incredulity as he asked, "What do you mean, 'had a connection to Balliol Croft?' "

"I don't want to get into that now. I think someone tried to kill you once. I'm also convinced that whoever killed Hart didn't act alone. One of the killers is now dead. There's at least one still on the loose. I simply want to urge you to be careful, Morris, while you're in Cambridge."

"And you think Balliol Croft somehow ties all this together?" The sandwich in front of Fain was going uneaten. Clearly the news he had just heard had given him a jolt. Fain had come to respect Spearman's intelligence and did not dismiss out of hand what he was hearing.

"I'm not sure. Telling you to be careful may be about as operative as when someone says, 'have a safe flight.' I mean, what do you do? Don't open the emergency door? Keep the stewardess off the pilot's lap? If I cannot tell you what to be careful of, I realize I'm not being very helpful. Maybe all I mean is, you have Balliol Croft, we've accomplished our objective, so now you should get your staff set up running the Marshall Institute, and you go back to Chicago. Maybe whoever does not want you to have Balliol Croft has given up or somehow secured his objective."

"Well, I can tell you one thing. I am feeling a lot less comfortable now than before we had this chat. All the same, I am not going to let this get to me. The Balliol Croft project still takes priority. When everything is set up the way I want it, then I'll return home and get back to my routine."

"Morris, that's a healthy attitude to have. I trust we'll remain in contact after Pidge and I get back to the States."

"I'll insist on it. You and Pidge must come to Chicago and be my guests at some point. I'd like to show my appreciation for what you have done for the foundation and, I hope, for future economic literacy. I'll take you out to the Stockyard Inn for the best steak you ever had."

"That sounds delightful."

Henry Spearman was glad Fain seemed relaxed again. He thought that if he continued this line of conversation, it would further relieve the distress that he might have caused his companion. "Is the Stockyard Inn really as good as everyone says?"

"I may be prejudiced, but it is my favorite restaurant in Chicago. I've been going there for years."

"Are you from Chicago originally?"

"Yes, my family is from there, and I've never left home. Except for college."

"I know you have the Fain Foundation. But is there a family business behind it? I don't think I've ever heard you say."

Fain, looking at ease, returned to his sandwich and coffee. "My family roots are very Chicago. Carl Sandburg and all that. That's why I know the Stockyard Inn. My father was in the beef business. And that's what I do now. In everyday terms, I run a slaughterhouse. I don't say that to many people. But you're an economist, and you understand free enterprise. I know you won't have a prejudice against what I do."

"A prejudice against it? Not at all. The beef business must be fascinating. So many different aspects. I recall reading that there are over a hundred different cuts of meat that consumers demand. And, of course, you sell the hides, too."

"Oh, certainly. We sell it all."

"Has your business been hurt by the recent concern over cholesterol? It would seem to me that the *Time* magazine cover story a few years ago about cholesterol's connection to heart attacks would provoke a drop in the demand for beef."

"I'm afraid so. We can't get the price we used to get. And, of course, as goes the price of beef, so goes the price of hides. Probably a good time to be in the shoe business."

As the two men talked, punters on the Cam poled their way upriver.

The trees around the Arbor House protected the diners from the noonday sun.

Spearman was intensely interested in what Fain was telling him about the beef business.

Henry Spearman and Morris Fain continued their conversation.

Chapter **24**:
Taking a Stand on Mathematical Bridge

The diminutive economist hoisted himself above the bridge's railing by placing his feet on the X-shaped cross members that supported it. His elbows rested on the wooden 6 × 6, his clasped hands extended over the river. Only a tall person could assume a contemplative posture at the railing of Mathematical Bridge. The balustrade was not constructed to accommodate observers from the bridge, at least not short ones. The medieval footbridge to Queens' College was designed to test the ingenuity of its architect, James Etheridge, who had wondered whether a wooden bridge could be built and remain standing without the use of nails, bolts, or staples. In 1749 he and its builder, James Essex, showed that it could.

The bridge then tested the ingenuity of several generations of Queensmen. The undergraduate at Queens' who disassembled the bridge out of love for science or for pranks (it was never clear which) could not find the secret of its proper reassembly. A frustrated University administration had finally bolted together the structure on which the Harvard professor was now standing.

Henry Spearman climbed half-way up the arch of the footbridge and stopped. He had not come to this particular site to see the cloister of Queens' or to observe the swans floating on the green river below. The drone of a plane overhead went unheard. Tourists passed behind him, going in either direction, without his taking notice. Spearman stood stock-still. He was deep in thought.

Spearman's mind surveyed the elaborate chain of events that had brought him to this melancholy state. His thoughts returned to his first meeting with Fain, the initial disappointment when Balliol Croft seemed lost, and his return home. Then the unsettling phone call. In spite of himself, he had been excited by the prospect of the Marshall Institute being renewed. Yet a heaviness was in his soul because of the eerie circumstances surrounding the reopening of the negotiations. It was not just Hart's death that bothered Spearman. His profession had lost a prominent member. True. But it was the cold-bloodedness of the crime, and the diabolical nature of the criminal brain that planned it, that troubled him most.

By applying the relentless logic of economic theory, Spearman had discovered the killer. But almost immediately, he found himself immersed in the throes of another even deeper mystery, all the more horrifying for Spearman because in finding the killer of Hart he had found a corpse. The murderess herself had met death at the hands of a murderer. Someone, it would seem, even more clever than she.

Today's lunch, pleasant as it was, had not salved Spearman's uneasiness. He stood motionless on the footbridge for over an hour, brooding. At times his thoughts were unfocused. He struggled for the insights that would bring clarity.

Eventually they came.

Spearman stepped down from the cross member of the Mathematical Bridge. He faced an oncoming stream of Italian schoolchildren who, with their teacher and guide, were on their way across the bridge and into Queens' College. Fending his way through the animated group of youngsters, Spearman picked up the pace when he took the short left to Silver Street. There he turned right and walked past Darwin College, crossed Queens' Road, and hurried up Sidgwick Avenue. When he had passed the Museum of Classical Archaeology, he turned right into the courtyard that took him to the Marshall Library. Spearman entered the building and hastily climbed the stairs to the card catalogue.

Within two minutes, Spearman sat alone at a long table with the book he had taken from the shelf. With the help of its index, he went immediately to the passage he sought. "Many of the most important cross connections between the values of different commodities are not obvious at first sight. Consider the case of things which cannot easily be produced separately; but are joined in a common origin, and may therefore be said to have a joint supply."

Spearman read on in Marshall's *Principles* for another page. He was satisfied.

Getting up from his chair, he returned the book and made his way to the circulation desk. "Excuse me, do you have a piece of stationery on library letterhead that you can spare?"

Henry returned to the McDonald home, where he met up with his wife following her visit to the Fitzwilliam Museum. "Pidge, I need your help with something. Jared isn't here, but I know he wouldn't mind if we made use of his dining room set."

The Spearmans moved to the small, oval-shaped, cherrywood table, where they seated themselves. Henry placed two sheets of paper before them. At the top of one was printed "The Marshall Library of Economics, University of Cambridge." The other was a sheet of Henry's personal stationery, on which he hurriedly scrawled a short message. He then signed his name. At this juncture, he looked up at his wife. "For this item, I need a feminine handwriting." Henry dictated a note which he requested Pidge to sign, not with her own name, but with the signature Mary Paley Marshall.

Chapter 25:
Grave Matters

A cemetery at midnight is the safest of places. Or so Henry Spearman believed as he passed the portals of St. Giles' cemetery. A burial ground held no fright for him. There was nothing deadly about the dead. The hoot of an owl, a wolf braying against the light of a full moon, the flutter of bats' wings in the night air— Spearman would be indifferent to these sounds whether he heard them in a cemetery or a wheat field.

These thoughts came into Henry Spearman's mind as he passed the portals of St. Giles' cemetery. There were no ghosts here. Great scholars, some of the greatest in the Western World, were buried on these grounds. That did not mean their spirits were hovering about. Alfred Marshall's burial plot was here. Spearman would have thought it preposterous that Marshall's ghost was at St. Giles' just because his mortal remains had been interred here. Marshall lived on in his writings, not in the form of some invisible specter.

Spearman swept his flashlight across the dirt pathway that went the length of the cemetery. He had been down this road before, but in the daylight. All he remembered was that if he took this route to the end, turned right, and made his way to the far south-west corner of the burial ground, he would reach the plot where Marshall was buried.

Without the assistance of his light, he could make out the shape of the funeral chapel nearby. This helped Spearman secure his bearings. He knew that soon he would be entering the graveyard proper. Spearman cast the beam in the direction of headstones on the right side of the path. The name George Edward Moore reflected back at him. Spearman walked on. Ludwig Wittgenstein, 1889–1951, became visible as he cast the light deeper into the yard. Spearman walked on. More names, but names he did not know: Courtney Stanhope Kelly, Raja Mohd Baqir Khan, Hugh MacAlister. The path made a right angle. Straight ahead was the wall that marked the back boundary line of St. Giles', and beyond it a garden. Walking slowly and methodically, Henry Spearman followed the pathway's turn. His light continued to play between the path and the tombstones. On his left, chiseled into a large pointed headstone: Frank Plumpton Ramsey (1903–1930).

Spearman paused and allowed his light to rest on the face of the tombstone. The stillness of the night was broken by what sounded like the snapping of a dry twig. Henry Spearman remained motionless, listening. He clicked off his flashlight and waited. Darkness, sudden and total, surrounded him.

Holding himself still, Spearman listened intently. His eyes began to grow accustomed to the night. Did he hear footsteps on the path behind him?

He thought it best not to use the flashlight any more. From now on, he would have to manage in the dark. Spearman placed the device in his pocket. He would need this later, he thought to himself. But not now. He continued his journey toward his destination in the farthest corner of the cemetery.

Spearman had been to the spot earlier. At the time he could not have anticipated that he would ever have to find his way back in the dark. In spite of his recollection of the site, he felt uncertain of himself when his feet left the path. Up until this point, he had been able to walk along an earthen track. But no longer. Now he was on the sod of the cemetery itself. Spearman reckoned he had traveled about fifteen feet from the Ramsey grave site. However, he knew the darkness might have confused him about the distance.

Then his foot struck a solid surface and Spearman found himself stumbling. He had to restrain himself from calling out. In the dark, his confusion turned to fear.

"Whumph."

Spearman took the brunt of the fall with his hands and forearms. Sharp pain raced up his shoulders. He silently cursed his clumsiness as he drew himself up on his hands and knees. His glasses were askew on his face, and he realized he had ripped the knees of his trousers. He searched to see if his flashlight remained in his pants pocket. It did. Spearman felt the palms of his hands. They were not bleeding, but they began to sting from the abrasions.

Spearman remained crouched until he had regained his composure. He searched the ground around him. After reaching to either side, he groped back to where he had first tumbled. To his right and left, and also by his feet, his hands felt a stone curb, about three inches high, protruding from the ground. This was the cause of his fall. Now Spearman knew where he was. The irony of it was slowly dawning upon him: this was Alfred Marshall's grave!

Spearman pulled himself up on one knee. He was no longer uncertain of his location in the burial yard, but he realized he did not want to remain there. Spearman stood up. There was a large yew tree a short distance to his left and he slowly moved in its direction. Positioning himself behind it, Spearman was now hidden from the spot where he had fallen.

Spearman rested against the trunk of the tree. He knew he might be in for a lengthy vigil. What he was there for could happen any time in the next few hours of darkness. The time for the watch had begun.

Spearman estimated two hours had passed since he had begun waiting. But there was no problem fighting fatigue. He was as alert as if it were the middle of the day. His eyes had become so acclimated to the dark that he could discern the shapes of tombstones when he looked out from behind his hiding place. All was still.

Then there was movement. At first, it was just an undulating white spot in the distance. To Spearman's eye, it appeared to be freely floating as if disembodied. The spot moved regularly from side to side, making no sound as it bobbed along the side of the cemetery.

Now Spearman could make out the beam. He fixed his eyes on the shaft of light, straining to see the figure guiding it. At this point, Spearman still heard nothing—except the sounds of his own heartbeat and labored breathing. Then he saw a figure slowly making its way up the dirt path, a flashlight's illumination marking the way. Where the path angled to the right, there was a pause. Spearman held his breath as he watched. Then the light pointed west, in his direction. Spearman secured his position behind the tree. He could not run the risk of the light's beam exposing him. Spearman would have to remain hidden until the light stopped where Spearman knew it would.

Now Spearman could hear the latest nocturnal visitor to St. Giles'. With the advantage of light, the figure moved more quickly than had Spearman. The padding of footsteps was all that Spearman heard at first. The footsteps stopped. A few minutes passed. Then came the sound that Spearman expected: half grating, half scraping. Spearman recognized it immediately. He knew he needed to wait. The fox was in the lair, but Spearman was going to let his prey dig his way into the trap. He rested his shoulder against the tree.

Spearman could not see his wristwatch. So he began counting silently to himself. He wanted about thirty minutes to pass. Spearman knew the longer he waited, the more fatigued his quarry would be, and the more definitive the evidence. Then it would be time to act.

The metallic sound of shovel against earth and stone continued without flagging. There was a rhythmic cadence as the ground was being spaded and as dirt was moved from within the rectangular curbstone to the outside.

Henry Spearman made his move.

"I hate to interrupt a man so dedicated to his labors. Quite an impressive performance. But grave desecration is the least of your talents. Murder—you're really good at that. Housebreaking? There's room for improvement. Conspiracy to murder? That may be your best production. And then there's fraud." Henry Spearman had stepped out from behind the tree, his flashlight shining steadily on the face of Morris Fain. "By the way, your labors here are in vain. Mary Marshall did not move the certificates. Neither have I."

At first Fain looked like a frightened deer caught in the headlights of an oncoming car. His right foot was frozen on the shoulder of the spade, his leg cocked, ready for the next dig. He realized there was no sense continuing. He released the shovel, leaving it protruding from the grave site.

"Henry, I'm amazed to see you here. And I'm embarrassed as well. I know that grave-robbing is a shameful thing. But when you sent me the note about the stock certificates being buried here, I fell victim to the temptation. I wanted to have them for Balliol Croft."

"You never stop, do you, Fain? I can see why you went into show business. Anyone who can act as convincingly as you would be able to organize first-rate productions. You'd recognize talent when you saw it." Spearman's light continued to play on Fain's face. Fain had picked up his own flashlight and shone it on Spearman in return. The beams crisscrossed in the dark.

"Henry, I don't know what you're talking about. But I do know you've got me all wrong. And if you'll come back to the Arbor House with me, I can prove it."

"I don't think so, Fain," Spearman replied brusquely. "I know you killed Dolores Tanner after arranging for her to murder Hart. Of course, the whole foundation deal was a scam. I realize now you'd stop at nothing to get Balliol Croft."

"It's a nice place, Henry, but Marshall's house is hardly something to kill for."

"Unless, as the infallible psalmist put it, 'wealth and riches shall be in his house.' In which case, the house has a value higher than its purchase price. Adam Smith drew the distinction between value in use and value in exchange. You also had drawn this distinction."

"What are you getting at?" Fain asked, perturbed. "I don't have time for your word games."

Spearman began walking toward Morris Fain. "You're right about one thing. Time has run out on you."

"Henry, don't be foolish. There still could be a good outcome from all this. And I mean for both of us. I'm talking millions here. You probably have no idea what those certificates are worth today. But I do. I've checked into it. They're worth nothing for silver, but they're worth a fortune in uranium. You and I are the only two people who know the secret of Balliol Croft. Tomorrow I get the title to the place. And access. We'll split the money from the sale of the certificates fifty-fifty. All we have to do is search the attic until we find them.''

"And how do we split the two murder raps? I suppose you'd like to make that fifty-fifty, as well." As he spoke, Spearman edged closer.

"You'd have nothing to worry about there. Tanner killed Hart. Tanner's dead. The police think I'm a target, not a suspect.''

"Ah, yes, the dumbbell in the punt. That really was an accident, wasn't it, Morris?''

"I suppose I owe that bit of luck to some careless student. But it kept the police from ever being on my trail.''

"Your proposition interests me." By this time, Spearman was face to face with Fain. "But there's one thing I need to know. I understand why you had to have Hart killed. But why did you kill Tanner?''

"I couldn't trust her. Eventually she might talk. Eventually she might have turned to blackmailing me. She thought she was in love with me. I strung her along for a while. The whole thing was unstable. Besides, Henry, believe me, she was a nothing. A cheap actress who never got over her father's death. I played on her desire for revenge. That's how I got her to kill Hart. Later I persuaded her to break into Balliol Croft to search the attic for the certificates. Unluckily, Thring returned and she had to get out before retrieving them.''

"What makes you think that *I* won't eventually blackmail you?''

"Oh, I'm sure of that," Fain responded. "And here's why!''

It was quick, but not totally unexpected. Fain wrested the shovel from the ground with both hands. Using a baseball grip on the handle, he lowered his shoulders and then ferociously swung the blade up and at Spearman's face. Had it struck Spearman as intended, the blow would have hit his head with the back of the blade.

But Spearman had taken a step back and raised his arm in defense. He took a hard, glancing shot with his shoulder. Moving backwards some more, his heels hit the curbstone that bordered Marshall's grave site, and again he lost his balance. He toppled backwards and cried out in the darkness.

Fain swung again in the direction where he expected his accuser to be. Not anticipating Spearman's fall, the shovel made an arc through the night air, its momentum twisting Fain into the position of a hitter who had just swung hard at an inside fastball. Spearman heard the swish of the blade above him. On hands and knees, he started scurrying across the ground. He could hear Fain cursing and slicing the air with the shovel's blade.

Spearman knew that his best ally was the darkness. By keeping low, he might elude the lethal swings intended for him. He scurried faster. His knees and hands felt hard ground and sharp gravel. His side brushed the rough granite edge of a tombstone. He wondered whether he ought to hide behind the marker. But he kept moving. Then his hands lost touch with the earth. He was in a void, but he couldn't stop. He plunged downward, head first, as if a trap door suddenly had given way under him.

Spearman lay flat on his back. He struggled to breathe, needed to gasp, but he feared for the noise he would make. In large gulps, he sucked in air. After catching his breath, he noticed the familiar smell.

"How convenient! A new grave ready for someone else's funeral tomorrow. You get to try it out first, Henry." Spearman looked up toward the voice but was blinded by the bright flashlight. The voice was clearly Fain's.

"You always liked choices, Professor. Here's your last one. Do you want to be buried alive? Or do you want to be clubbed into unconsciousness before the burying begins? Or are you indifferent?"

Before Spearman could respond, he felt the first spadeful of earth fall on his legs. Desperately he tried to rise. Then he realized that he needed to stay out of reach of a blow from Fain's shovel. The dirt was falling faster. It dawned on Spearman that the sides of the grave would make it difficult for someone his height to escape, even without an opponent above. A mass of earth fell on his head. Spearman instinctively put his arms over his face, expecting the next load to fall there.

It never did.

From above, there was the sound of a sharp crack followed by a heavy thump on the ground. Then Spearman again saw a bright light shining down on him. "Are you all right, Professor Spearman?"

This time the voice behind the light was friendly and eager. Spearman's fears began to subside. "I think so, Steve. I'm bruised but alive. What happened up there?"

"I broke a paddle over Fain's head. He never heard me come up behind him. He was too busy trying to bury you. I hit him very hard. I think he'll need a doctor. But I'm more worried about you."

Pipes reached down to pull Spearman from the freshly dug grave that had almost become the professor's tomb. Spearman warmly embraced the young man who had rescued him. "You did good work, Steve. I'm indebted to you."

"I owe you thanks, too," Pipes replied. "After all, I'm the one who came to you for help when the police thought I killed Dolores. When you told me your plan and asked for my help, I was relieved. I knew if it worked I'd no longer be a suspect. My hiding out here seemed the least I could do to help. So all of the thanks should go to you. Anyway, I had a scare, too. When you stopped at Ramsey's tomb, I wasn't sure if it was you or Fain who'd arrived first. Stupid me, I made a noise then. But when you walked on, I realized it was you and I hoped you realized it was me."

Spearman gave Steve's arm a pat. "There was a second when I felt a bit jumpy. But I knew the Ramsey grave is where we agreed you'd hide. So I assumed the noise came from you. Anyway, we'd better get moving. We don't know how badly Fain is hurt. If it's bad, we need to get help for him. If it isn't bad, I don't want to have to battle him again."

Spearman hesitated only briefly. "Here's what I propose. I've a car parked down Huntingdon. I'll go there and drive to the police station and get help. You wait here with Fain. If he comes to . . . well, after all, you have the comparative advantage."

Chapter 26:
Professor Spearman Professes

"Benedicto Benedictur."

With no Master present, the most senior Fellow at Bishop's intoned the grace that always ended High Table at the College's dining hall. Spencer Hatwood, to whom these duties had fallen, had heard the prayer so often that he knew it from memory. But unlike Nigel Hart, who recited with perfunctory speed, the elderly biology scholar spoke each word of the benediction distinctly.

As soon as Hatwood was finished, Mr. Pinn struck the cymbal that stood by the doorway through which the Fellows came and went from High Table. At the deep sound of the gong, the undergraduates rose in unison while the faculty made their exit, single file, into the hallway that led to the Senior Common Room.

As he followed Jared McDonald, Spearman wondered how Harvard undergraduates would react to an etiquette rule that required them to rise when their teachers entered to dine and rise again when they left. During the meal, students would observe the faculty eating, unapproachable, seated at a table elevated above them, being elegantly served.

Outside the dining room, the assembly entered a large walk-in closet where Fellows at the College had been assigned individual hooks for the academic gowns they wore to dinner. As a guest, Spearman had been lent a robe—there always were extra gowns, since not every Fellow dined at the College every night. Spearman had found himself wearing a black habiliment whose sleeve length made eating his soup difficult. He was relieved to place it back on its owner's hook.

Spearman was aware that High Table at Cambridge was a prelude to an even longer part of the evening ceremony. After dessert was served in the hall, Fellows and their guests moved into the Senior Common Room for brandy and port or, for an increasing number of Fellows, simply coffee. The potables were ancillary to the evening's discussion among the scholars. At High Table you could talk readily only with the person across from you and on either side. In the Senior Common Room, one's words could be shared with a larger audience.

Retiring to the Senior Common Room was not mandatory for High Table participants. Indeed, married life among Bishop's Fellows had taken its toll on the number in attendance. But tonight all those at High Table made their way toward the high-ceilinged room at the end of Bishop's dining hall.

As the Fellows shuffled through the passageway leading to the room where they would reassemble, Delmore Vine edged alongside Henry Spearman. "Professor Spearman, I can't tell you how pleased I am that you've agreed to join us tonight. It will be a welcome change from the topic that's dominated the discussion for weeks."

"What was the hot topic?" Spearman asked of the junior Fellow.

"Who will replace Hart as Master of Bishop's," Vine replied. "That's about the only thing that's been on everyone's mind. People gossip about it almost incessantly. But, of course, I'm sure you're not surprised at that. It's what you would expect."

"I'm sure you are right. But I can't honestly say that it is what I would expect. We don't have the position of Master in the States. I suppose the closest thing we have is a dean. People do worry about who will be selected for that position. But I never get involved in those discussions."

"Why not? Surely you care about their credentials and qualifications. And their background." Vine had a puzzled look on his face.

"As far as I am concerned, there are two—and only two—

qualifications for dean. They are, one, does the candidate *know* me? And two, does the candidate *like* me?''

Delmore Vine was silent for a moment as he tried to determine how Spearman's criteria for a dean might apply to the selection of a new Master. Then its wisdom became blindingly clear. ''I see your point,'' he murmured.

A circle of chairs awaited the group as it entered. After everyone was seated, the butler made the initial serving of drinks and coffee. This ended Mr. Pinn's working day. Thereafter, it would be the job of the most junior Fellow present to see that glasses were kept filled and the bar tab accurately recorded against the proper Fellow's account.

This evening Henry Spearman had been invited to High Table by Jared McDonald. McDonald was encouraged to do so by virtually every Fellow at Bishop's. His friend's sudden popularity had nothing to do with any change in viewpoints on economic policy on the part of the faculty. Rather, it was due to a curiosity so consuming that it overcame even ideological divisions. Everyone wanted to hear firsthand Spearman's account of his adventure the night before.

''McDonald, old chap, I hope you'll see fit to have your friend Spearman to Table tonight.'' This from a Fellow who had not been cordial to McDonald in years.

''Now listen, old man, it would be a pleasure for me to invite your friend Spearman to be my guest this evening. Unless, of course, you've already made arrangements to invite him yourself.'' This from a Fellow who had not invited a guest in years.

''McDonald, will you by any chance be bringing Dr. Spearman along with you to High Table today? I'm only inquiring because it would affect my decision whether to be there.'' This from an elderly Fellow who seldom attended.

''Jared, I understand this is your friend Spearman's last day in Cambridge. Surely you plan to have him at High Table tonight for a proper send–off.'' And this from Olivia Hale!

Pidge Spearman was seated between G. Shepherd and her husband. All three were the guests of Jared McDonald, who was to their left. McDonald wanted to be with the Spearmans on the night before their departure, and although he was not a close friend of G. Shepherd's, he felt the book dealer was a kindred spirit. Spearman, after all, had cleared both of them of any suspicion in Hart's death. It seemed appropriate that Shepherd be invited. He accepted on the spot.

Also present as a guest was Duncan Thring. Although he was a Fellow at St. John's, tonight Thring had been invited at Henry Spearman's insistence, to hear the account of an affair of which his home was the focal point. He was seated between Chandler and Olivia Hale. Both Thring and Olivia Hale had been friends of Hart's. They sat directly across the circle of chairs from the Spearmans and G. Shepherd.

When Ajit Chandavarkar raised his voice, thereby hushing the conversations of others in the circle, Malcolm Dallenbach was relieved that his colleague had broken the ice, and he knew the others felt similarly. "Henry," said Chandavarkar," I know I can speak for all of us when I say how indebted we are to you. And I want to express our sorrow not only for the inconvenience you have undergone—well, it really goes beyond inconvenience—we can all see that you have suffered physical harm. What you did went beyond any duty you might have felt you owed a college, especially one not your own. Even so, I feel it necessary to call on you for one more service to us. Although we know that the instigator of the murder of our much-lamented Master has been apprehended—an accomplishment that even the police admitted might not have occurred without your labors—we remain in the dark about almost every detail. The authorities thus far have been most parsimonious in providing information, even though we in this room have been the ones most adversely affected by Nigel's death. Would you allow us to ask a few questions of you? Perhaps then the what, when, and wherefores that now plague us would be cleared up to our relief." Chandavarkar sat back in his chair. The appreciative nods from his colleagues did not go unnoticed by him.

Henry Spearman cleared his throat before responding.

"I have always believed that a professor should be willing to profess. I'll try to satisfy your request, Ajit, but let me hasten to add that I take no particular satisfaction from having done the things for which you have credited me. I do not say this out of modesty. As my wife would tell you, modesty is not my strong suit. I say it out of a deeply felt belief that what I did would have been done by anyone who took economics seriously. And for that I can take no credit for myself. It was the greats of the discipline, from Smith to Marshall, who taught me that economics is a way of thinking. Now, I do not know how to think any other way.

"I think I can be of most help to you if I make you aware, or remind you as the case may be, that Alfred Marshall ventured to the state of Nevada. This was in 1875—the American West depicted in cowboy movies. We do not know many of the details about his time there. But we do know Marshall visited silver mines in Virginia City. Apparently, he purchased stock in one called the Mad Hatter. Marshall later came to understand that these shares were virtually worthless, and he treated the certificates more like souvenirs than claims on real assets. In time, long after Marshall's death, these pieces of paper came to be worth millions. After Evensong two nights ago, I called my broker in the States. He told me something consistent with my expectations. Uranium had been discovered in the mine. If Marshall had purchased only one share of that stock in 1875, that single share in today's dollars would be worth about seven hundred and fifty thousand dollars. We know that the Hesketh girl played with several certificates. It was this wealth that played the same role for Morris Fain that the apple played for Adam in the Garden: irresistible temptation. But there is one major difference between the two stories. In Eden, Eve tempted Adam. In Cambridge, Adam tempted Eve.

"Fain became acquainted with Dolores Tanner when she was touring with a theatrical group in the States. They met in Chicago. During this time, he learned from her that as a little girl she had been in Alfred Marshall's home when her father was visiting with Marshall's widow, Mary Paley Marshall. Mrs. Marshall, to entertain the little girl, gave her a few things to play with. Among them were some colorful pieces of paper. The Hesketh girl hid these under the floorboard in the attic—not thinking to steal them, but more as an act of girlish mischief. She had hoped to play with them again. They had an unusual name which the little girl associated with a favorite story. But she never returned to retrieve them.

"Years later, when she happened to describe this incident to Morris Fain, he knew at once that the hidden pieces of paper were the stock certificates in the Mad Hatter mine. Being an avid reader of financial newspapers and journals, he realized they were valuable and devised a scheme for retrieving them. His idea was to buy Balliol Croft, the way an oil company buys land from the hardscrabble farmer who doesn't know he's sitting on a gusher.

"Nigel Hart unknowingly upset this plan. So Fain played his trump card. He knew from Miss Tanner that she had a deep-seated grudge against Hart. Hart had been an Apostle, and she thought that he had been responsible for her father's death. Her father was Andrew Hesketh, a promising economist here some years back, who committed suicide after being blackballed from the Apostles by Hart.

"Hart's guilt or innocence isn't the question here. What matters is that Miss Tanner believed he was responsible for her father's death and its consequences for her. Fain persuaded her to move to Cambridge to kill Hart, playing on her bitterness and helping her plan the murder. The Saltmarsh residence provided a front, covering her real reason for being in the Cambridge area. With Hart out of the way, he figured he would have access again to Balliol Croft." Henry Spearman pointed to Duncan Thring. "Fain was pretty certain you'd be ready to sell to him at that point."

Thring nodded in agreement. "We-we-well, after all, he was my ne-next best alternative."

"Yes, to an anatomist. In any event," Spearman went on, "Fain figured he was home free. The police had not solved Hart's murder. And, quite by luck, Fain not only wasn't a suspect, but there was concern that he might be the next victim."

"Why the next victim?" Chandler Hale wanted to know.

"Oh, I thought all of you had heard about the accident Morris Fain had his first day in Cambridge. He was on a punt near St. John's when a dumbbell fell from a College window and narrowly missed hitting him. It was a potentially deadly accident. The police investigated but never were able to nail down what happened. I thought it was probably an accident. My wife, on the other hand, had her suspicions. However, after Hart's death, I had to entertain the possibility that whoever killed Hart also tried to kill Fain. There was the Balliol Croft connection. Of course, this misled me completely. Even after I realized that Miss Tanner had killed Hart."

"You've made quite clear why she did it. But you haven't

explained how you could have known she did it," Olivia Hale intervened. "I assume it wasn't just a lucky guess."

"There was no need to guess. Her behavior gave her away. Let me explain and, of course, the economists present will realize how obvious it was.

"My wife and I had been invited to see Grantchester. All very innocent. We had met a wonderful young man who had taken us for a punt ride. He urged us to come and see him in Grantchester, where he lived, and we decided to do so. That was just four days ago. While we were there my wife and I met Dolores Tanner for the first time. Nice personality, attractive and pleasant. She lived in the same boarding house as the young man we had gone to see. He was the one who introduced us. She was concerned that our car had blocked hers in, and that brought her car to my attention. I had seen the car before. In fact, Professor Hale, it was pointed out to me on my way to your party. The car belonged to Nigel Hart. It still had the Bishop's sticker on it."

"Surely, Professor Spearman, the fact that Miss Tanner bought the Master's car did not suggest to you that she killed him. She bought the vehicle, after all; she didn't steal it."

"Exactly. She bought it. That's the point. Had she stolen it, I'd have had nothing to go on."

Spearman's audience did some exchanging of puzzled glances and shrugging of shoulders.

Spearman continued his story. "The young man who was to show us around—Steven Pipes is his name—was telling us about how Dolores Tanner had acquired the car. He indicated she was totally uninterested in an opportunity to buy the same make and model at virtually the same price from a close friend of his, a car he knew to be of high quality. Pipes even kidded her in front of us that she had forgone this alternative, and instead purchased an automobile off a used-car lot. That was the car I recognized as the one Hart used to have.

"I felt uneasy at the time. But before I could think about the matter, Pipes had me and my wife hiking through Grantchester. Later that evening at Jared's home, the uneasiness returned. That's when I thought through what I had heard and made the connection between Tanner buying the car and my wife's mother buying insurance. And then it became clear, as I suspect you can see."

"I'll confess I don't. Perhaps I'm the only person in this room who doesn't. What does insurance for your mother-in-law have to do with Tanner buying the Master's car?" Malcolm Dallenbach believed he was speaking for others more reticent to admit their lack of comprehension.

"In economics, there is a theory of asymmetric information. As applied to used cars, it goes like this: you can be quite certain that the cars on a secondhand lot consist mainly of 'lemons,' as we say in the States. The people who have good cars to sell know that because buyers have less information about a car's quality than sellers do, buyers will not recognize the superior quality of these cars. Unable to recognize their quality, people shopping at a used-car lot are understandably unwilling to take the risk of paying a premium price for what might turn out to be a clunker. Because sellers of well-maintained used cars would find their vehicles selling for no more than poorly maintained cars on a secondhand lot, the best used cars are sold privately. The ones remaining have a higher probability of being lemons.

"Insurance markets have the same problem. By similar reasoning, this problem of asymmetric information leads to adverse selection; that is, the good risks pay too much, the bad risks not enough. This means more bad risks get insured than good risks. That's the adverse selection.

"Dolores Tanner had the opportunity to skirt this problem. But she didn't take it. That's when I knew she had an ulterior motive for getting Hart's car. But what could it be? I knew the murder weapon had never been found. Tanner's behavior made sense if Hart's car contained the hastily concealed murder weapon. Pipes thought she was hot-headed; I knew she was cold-blooded."

Gregory Shepherd took advantage of the pause in Spearman's story. "Jared McDonald and I, and your friend Pipes, of course, are the beneficiaries of your detective work, Professor Spearman. You released us from all suspicion. It has been pleasant not having the police examining my shop and watching where I go. What I don't understand is how you knew I did not kill Hart before you determined that Miss Tanner did. You were in my shop before you met her. *I* knew at the time I didn't kill Hart. But how could you have known that?"

"As I told you at the time, you had nothing to gain; and you lost a friend. You had costs with no offsetting benefits."

"Wait a minute, Henry, I know Shepherd is innocent, but you forget that he got all of Hart's books which he promptly began selling—and some at substantial prices." Jared McDonald had leaned forward in his chair and turned to his right in order to look past G. Shepherd and Pidge Spearman, who were seated between him and his friend.

"I never believed that Shepherd was involved in Hart's death. I came to that conclusion in your home right after you were informed—by someone named Gabor, I believe?—that Shepherd had been picked up by the police. You indicated that he might be in real trouble because he had benefited from Hart's demise. But then it turned out that he hadn't benefited at all."

"But he got his books...."

"Yes, at market prices. You told me yourself that they were auctioned off to the highest bidder. Other bidders would know what the books were worth at retail. They would bid the price up to where Shepherd, as the successful bidder, would earn no excess returns on his purchase. Later, when I visited Mr. Shepherd's shop, he confirmed that he had to compete with other booksellers and dealers for the Hart library. This was just another example of competition equalizing returns. I also observed that Mr. Shepherd did not derive pleasure from possessing Hart's books. To him, they were inventory. He was eager to see them sold in order to recover his investment."

Ajit Chandavarkar spoke up. "Very persuasive, Henry. But I have a rather indelicate question to ask of you. Quite frankly, a number of my colleagues,—and you'll pardon my saying so, McDonald, that I was among them—felt it quite possible that Hart's death had political motivation. It is no secret that economics here at Cambridge is split along ideological grounds. Nigel Hart was prominently identified with one camp. I think it is fair to say— and I mean this as a compliment—that McDonald would be identified as Hart's counterpart on the other side. In Hart's absence, McDonald's group has one less opponent. It was conceivable, wasn't it, that one of them executed a plan to get rid of Hart?"

Olivia Hale extended a compliment to the colleague seated on her left: "Dr. Chandavarkar has just shot my fox. I had hoped to ask the same thing myself."

"I am well aware of the divisions that exist at Cambridge University. I have no doubt that they are deep and real. But I dismissed free market economists as suspects in Nigel Hart's death for the very same reason I would dismiss Marxo-Keynesians. Neither side had anything to gain. Hart's death did not tip the balance of power to either side's advantage." Spearman stopped and gave a twitch of his shoulders, accompanied by a dismissive gesture with his hands. "Look, you have to remember that the key to analyzing these problems is not scrutinizing motives—that's where the police so often go wrong—but scrutinizing gains and losses.

"The hour is getting late, and Pidge and I have an early departure for Heathrow. But I don't want to leave you in the dark. What ultimately pointed the finger at Morris Fain was Alfred Marshall. There is a certain irony, I suppose, in that it was the original owner of Balliol Croft who gave Fain's secret away. Fain had told me from the start that he was in the beef business. Hides and beef, actually, because you don't produce one without the other. And yet when I asked him the simplest question about a drop in the demand for beef, he answered by saying this would cause a decrease in the price of hides. Well, anybody who has read Marshall knows that is a mistake. Marshall used that exact example."

At this point, McDonald looked straight across the circle of chairs at Olivia Hale and interjected: "Marshall also used the example of wheat and straw and made the same point because they are produced jointly as well. He showed how a decrease in the demand for straw led to less wheat being planted, meaning less wheat would be available in the market. This pushed up the price of wheat. Much to the distress of the poor, I might add." Jared McDonald gave Olivia Hale a polite smile.

Spearman continued. "When I realized Fain was not who he claimed to be, I told this to Pidge. She reminded me of something she had learned at the Hales' party following my lecture. Graham Carlton, who was a guest at the party, had indicated to my wife that he knew a Morris Fain in the theater business in Chicago. A playbill in Dolores Tanner's possessions placed her in Chicago. Not hard to put two and two together there.

"That's when I decided to set my trap for Mr. Fain. I sent him a note, to which I attached a copy of another note that was a fake. The fake attachment was on stationery from the Marshall Library, purportedly in the handwriting of Mary Paley Marshall. It stated that she had found the mining certificates and had buried them in the same plot with her husband. I had no doubt at all that Morris Fain would attempt to retrieve those stocks. A man who is willing to murder will not stop at graverobbing. I also had no doubt that he would do so last night. Today was the day he would owe Duncan Thring the balance due on Balliol Croft. If he found the certificates earlier, he would lose only his downpayment while he was millions richer. As I expected he would, Fain showed up, as you can see from the bandages I'm wearing. If it were not for Steve Pipes being with me, I would have joined the ranks of those distinguished Cambridge scholars currently in repose at St. Giles'.

"I would say that the person most indebted to me in this room is not anyone associated with Bishop's College but with St. John's. Duncan, those certificates probably are still under the floorboards of your attic. In the States, there is an expression: 'possession is nine-tenths of the law.' If that holds in England, you are a very wealthy man."

"I'm afraid that in England, P-P-Professor Spearman, taxes are nine-tenths of your possessions. You've made Her Mah-M-Majesty's Government quite a bit wealthier." The quick retort of Duncan Thring provoked laughter around the circle, none louder than that of Olivia Hale.

As the evening at Bishop's Senior Common Room was drawing to a close, Jared McDonald asked, "What's next for you, Henry, when you get back to the States? Less excitement, I trust."

"Oh, you know how it is when you travel," Spearman replied with a look of resignation. "When I get back, the mail will be stacked up, my secretary will give me a pile of phone messages, and I've got two research projects under way."

"Remember, Henry," Pidge chimed in, "you've promised to lecture this summer in Israel and you have that Montreal conference in August. I hope you won't take on anything more for awhile. As it is now, you'll never get everything done."

"But that's to be expected, Pidge. Besides, as a great sage once said, 'life consists mainly of unfinished business.' "